...'m blinking in ... s
... d ent. A ... get
... again before ... nat a
... where are ...
... one witch on ... on ...

Not a sound penetrate... ... I hear a
whisper from somewhere ... high above me. I hear the
voice again. It's Paul. Only his voice seems to be floating
off the highest part of the ceiling, as if he . . . It's just Paul
being silly. I know that. But it's as if I also know something else, something bad, for dark forces are gathering
round me. And a picture's forming but I don't want to see
it. I won't see it. A shiver slices through me and I shudder,
swaying backwards as the room blurs and fades away. I
never actually pass out, yet I come close, standing right on
the border. But I manage to keep dimly aware of the three
pairs of hands anxiously clamouring round me ... h so
gently depositing me in the wicker chair. Then I hear Paul
say, 'We must do something,' and he sounds so concerned
a smile creeps across my lips.

'I'm all right,' I gasp.

But I'm not all right.

Pete Johnson

We, the Haunted

MAMMOTH

First published in Great Britain 1989
by William Collins Sons & Co. Ltd
Published 1993 by Mammoth
an imprint of Reed International Books Ltd
Michelin House, 81 Fulham Road, London SW3 6RB
and Auckland, Melbourne, Singapore and Toronto

Reprinted 1994 (twice), 1995

ISBN 0 7497 1453 0

A CIP catalogue record for this title
is available from the British Library

Printed and bound in Great Britain
by Cox & Wyman Ltd, Reading, Berkshire

To my sister who appeared on
'Blind Date' and my mother who hasn't yet!

Contents

Part One – By Caro   1
Two Months Later   19

Part Two – By Caro:
Two Weeks Later   37

Part Three:
Chapter One – By Dean   46
Chapter Two – By Caro   56
Chapter Three – By Dean   67
Chapter Four – By Dean   73
Chapter Five – By Dean   85
Chapter Six – By Caro   92
Chapter Seven – By Dean   100
Chapter Eight – By Dean   107
Chapter Nine – By Dean   114

Part Four – By Caro:
Four Months Later   125

With thanks to those stars of Drama Lessons past: Kevin Foord, Mandi Lee, Peter Brown, Greg Hodgson and to all those current stars of English, Drama and Media Studies at Stevenage College.

Love to Dodie Smith – who wrote the screenplay for one of the cinema's great ghost stories – 'The Uninvited' and to Dulcie Gray.

Special thanks to Rosemary Sandberg and Carol Watson for their perceptive analyses and invaluable support.

Part One – by Caro

I open my eyes. No need to peer at my watch. I know what time it is.

It's two o'clock in the morning. I recognise the strange, hushed silence and the darkness. The dark is at its deepest now. You can feel it folding down on to you. For this time belongs only to the dark. I shouldn't be awake now. No one should. No one is. Nothing stirs, nothing except . . .

Just where do the shadows come from? The shadows which appear out of the air, the ones we call ghosts. And especially the ghost in my attic. The ghost we both saw.

If only ghosts survived into daylight. Then we could see them clearly – and know they weren't just dreams. Just dreams! What a silly thing to write. For nothing is stronger than a dream. Nothing!

And as soon as I close my eyes I know what dream will be there waiting for me. It's always the same dream: I go back. I can't stop going back. It happened some time ago and everyone tells me to leave it behind in the past and get on with my life now! So I pretend I have forgotten. I never speak of it and they're happy.

But I don't want to lose those days – ever. I close my eyes tightly. Any second now I'll be there again, back to one Friday night, where it started most unexpectedly . . .

* * *

We're edging closer together every minute. Until we can't get much closer. From all sides Vicky – my best friend since infant school – and I are surrounded. Guys in black leather jackets and studded wristbands and big biking boots and metal shin-pads circle us disbelievingly – and look behind us for our space-ship.

But it's the girls who are making with the bad eye. There are clumps of them, all wearing black leather mini skirts and black leggings down to the ankles. Out here we're just possibly safe but I won't be making any trips to the Ladies tonight. I told Vicky not to wear her blue stripy dress. Not that my pink jersey exactly helps either. We've marked ourselves out as invaders – but then how were we to know that everyone here would be Gothics – we've never been here before. This expedition was all Vicky's idea – but my fault.

You see, recently I've developed a disturbing new habit, I've started leaving parties early. I can't explain why because I love parties – or rather, I love being invited to them. And I'll admit I love the dressing up too. It's just the parties themselves . . . I mean, I do make an effort, giving off gallons of party spirit but inside me there's this horrible feeling of emptiness and sadness. It starts off very tiny, just a vague, niggly whisper of sadness but it gnaws away at me and grows pretty fast until finally . . . Well, if you want to know, I ran out of my last party, which is a pretty nerdy thing to do. Yes, I know.

Anyway, Vicky gave me a talking to and decided I was suffering from a 'jaded palate' and her prescription was a new experience, like going somewhere I've never been before. We planned a visit to a ritzy nightclub in London's West End. We ended up at a local youth club watching a talent competition called BATTLE OF THE BANDS, only it should have been retitled A GOTHIC CONVENTION.

'We could be even more out of place,' says Vicky. 'I might have worn my white boots with the tassels.'

'Or what about my leopard-skin trousers!'

Vicky and I started giggling and acting all Sharonish – because that's how we feel.

Laughing becomes harder though, as the black uniforms engulf us. It's as if I'm in a long dark tunnel with the only splash of bright colour bouncing off the stage. I stand watching the yellows, pinks and violets exploding over the audience like fireworks and willing Vicky to say: 'Let's go home.' I don't want to say it, as that'd sound ungrateful.

Finally though, boredom wins out over politeness and I whisper:

'Shall we go? What do you think?' But my question is drowned by a sudden surge of dark shapes into the middle of the floor. Dance music is now splattering out of the amplifiers. And before I can repeat my question we are being chatted up.

'I've got a problem and a proposition. I have two left feet and need to learn to dance. So which one of you beautiful girls is going to teach me?'

I look up and then back down again, groaning inwardly. I know him. He's called Bosh and he's an idiot. Last time I saw him he had this huge blonde Mohican. He's been round my house. I remember we measured his Mohican – 21 centimetres. And, my dad hated him.

'How many more of these cockerels are you bringing round?' he moaned.

But he needn't have worried. Bosh never rang me, as he'd promised. I wasn't too sorry. People with freaky haircuts are rarely as much fun as you think they'll be.

Only now, Bosh has lacquered his hair down – but as he's got no hair on the sides and back of his head he looks like a judge with a wig on. And a jerk.

Yet, Vicky's smiling at him. It's a 'just to keep in

3

practice' smile. Usually Vicky'd be surrounded by admirers by now as she's very striking looking, with long naturally wavy blonde hair and a figure I'd kill for. Tonight though, no one's approached Vicky and she's showing definite withdrawal symptoms, so . . .

I hope it's just one dance. I want to go home. But Vicky and Bosh return giggling and he keeps touching her fingernails. I make conversation while scrutinising Vicky. She likes him. That's my cue:

'I've just seen someone I know so I'll see you later.'

For the first time Bosh acknowledges my existence: 'Haven't we met before?' he croaks in a 'I meet so many people' tone.

'You'd have remembered me if we had,' I reply, then I dive away trying to look as if I'm going somewhere. The trick is to walk very quickly. The only problem with this is you end up nowhere even faster.

Added to which, the dance floor is getting pretty crowded with male Gothics. They dance by either standing completely still and waving their hands wildly in the air, or by jumping into the air and head butting each other. Neither seems in the least safe for spectators. So I decide to adjourn to the safety of the bar while I wait for Vicky. We always wait for each other – and usually it's me who does the waiting. I don't mind, much, except I feel awkward and vulnerable here.

I begin ducking and pushing my way through to the doorway and then freeze, as if suddenly hypnotised. Standing in the doorway are two boys. The first has got on a long black coat, John Lennon-style glasses and a frown – but my eyes fasten on the second boy.

He's wearing a black peakless cap, a black jacket and blue jeans with turn-ups. There are plenty of boys dressed like that – but this one is different. Spellbound, I watch him talking and the way he keeps smiling, a wide, generous

4

smile. He looks like he could be a magic laugh. His face is funny too, attractive rather than good-looking but there's something about his face which holds you.

I should turn away now. Forget him. He's just a face in the crowd passing by. Turn away. Go on. It's rude to stare. Very rude. But I can't turn away from him. And I go on staring until I catch his eye. He's looking at me now. This is the moment I pretend I'm really peering at something else . . . go on, look away. I intend to. But my eyes never leave him. It's as if they're glued to where he's standing.

All at once he's strolling towards me. I watch him edge through the dancers. But they're blurred and fuzzy, all I see is *him* getting nearer and nearer, his eyes still set firmly upon me. I'm shivering with excitement. This is crazy and silly and I feel so wonderful . . .

He's right in front of me. He grins that cheeky, melting smile. And then he touches my arm – a ripple of pleasure passes through me – and leads me into the dancing.

He's a lithe, supple dancer, actually swinging his arms to a set rhythm. I try and copy the hand-jiving that I've seen the other girls doing here. But I soon give up and just stare back up at him. He's still smiling.

The band finishes, normal yellow lights beam down while the next band clamours into action. I look round for Vicky. I can't see her. A little knot forms in my stomach. Who is this guy? And just exactly what am I doing?

'Would you like a drink?' and his voice cracks as he asks me.

I sense he's nervous too. That relaxes me a little. We go into the bar. He hands me a white beaker of coke, that's all they're serving. I sip it, just for something to do. It's flat.

'Anything to eat?'

I shake my head. He must think I'm a right floosie staring at him like that. What's got into me?

'I'm Paul,' he says.

'I'm Caroline – but all my friends call me Caro.'

'Hello, Caro,' he says. His eyes are still lingering over my face as if he really likes what he sees.

'Your cap – it's good. Did you cut the peak off yourself?' I ask.

'Yeah, it kept getting in the way. So I cut it off.'

For some reason we both smile inanely at this.

'Just like Heaven,' he says.

'What?'

'That song they're playing: "Just Like Heaven" by The Cure. Sorry, I really like The Cure. What music do you like?'

My mind goes blank. 'Oh, all sorts really.'

He leans forward: 'See that guy over there?' He points to a greying man in a suit who's one of the judges. 'Did you ever see such wicked flares? He should be deported for wearing flares like that.' Then he breaks into a laugh – he laughs the way they do on cartoons. I mean, his whole face laughs. His eyes pop out of his head and his smile seems to stretch down to his shoulders. It's weird – but nice and highly infectious.

That laugh keeps taking over Paul as we work through the ritual questions. We're both in the fifth year. He goes to Norsfield Boys, I'm at Carter Mixed. He's got two older brothers and one younger one, with whom he has to share a room – which he hates. I've got two younger sisters and my own attic. He says he wishes he had his own place . . . But it's our eyes that do most of the talking.

In fact, it's like I'm on two separate planes at once: there's one part of me that's sitting in a dingy bar with a beaker of dead coke in my hand, then there's another part of me that's floating and feels so high and happy – so incredibly happy.

'You seeing anyone special at the moment?'

6

Paul asks the question in such an exaggeratedly casual way my heart turns a small somersault.

'No, not especially. How about you?'

Before he can reply, the guy in the black coat is back. Paul introduces us: 'Caro, this is Dean – Dean, this is Caro.'

Dean scowls and then proceeds to scrutinise me as if he's standing a long distance away and trying to get me into focus. I don't think he likes me.

Soon more people gather round Paul. He seems to know just about everyone here. They're all yarning on about the competition which has apparently just finished. Dean's got his back to me now and is proclaiming: 'Did you hear that guitar solo? He was all over the place. And what about the bass?'

I'm being swamped by all this activity round Paul. I can't even see him properly now.

'So here you are.' Vicky steams over. 'Sorry, sorry, sorry for being so long but I've . . . Well, I'll tell you on the way. Ready to go then?' I nod my head towards Paul. But Vicky doesn't understand. How can I explain that I've been having an intimate evening with that guy in the middle of the crowd and I . . . No, I certainly couldn't tell Vicky that. Yet I can't just slip away. Paul hasn't even got my phone number. But Vicky's already springing out of the bar. I stand up and instantly Paul stands up too and is beside me.

'I want to ask you something,' he says. 'But I can't say it here.'

By now Vicky has turned back. I make the introductions. And Paul says, 'It's great meeting you, Vicky, but will you excuse us a minute – we've got to see a man about a penguin.' He then propels me past Vicky and outside.

'Sorry about that, but if I don't say this now I never will.'

Paul gives a nervous cough, 'I can talk better in the dark. I am a creature of the night, you see. Anyhow, here goes – what would you say if I invited you to a party with me tomorrow?'

I count to four, just to at least try and disguise my enthusiasm. A plane drones overhead and there's some loud tuneless singing behind us – but none of that matters. What matters is . . .

'Yeah, why not – I'll give it a bash,' I say.

'Great!' he exclaims.

I think he really likes me. That's handy, because I really like him – even though I don't quite know why.

We exchange phone numbers, suddenly both nervous again. Saying 'yes' when a boy asks you out is a real conversation stopper.

'Till tomorrow night then,' I say.

'Yeah, what's your name again?'

'What?'

'Joke. No, I can't wait. See you in about twenty hours, Caro – Oh, Caro?'

'Yes.'

'It's a beard party.'

'What's that?'

'No. Stay cool. You'll love it. And I've got just the beard for you.'

'You *are* joking, aren't you?' I call after him.

But he's already gone and all I hear swirling towards me is his laughter.

II

I'm wearing a large orange beard while drinking through a straw and talking to a girl who has sellotaped a blonde hairpiece on to her chin. My beard is hot, clammy and very itchy but this is one party I'm really enjoying. Perhaps because it's such a good laugh and everyone's far friendlier than at a normal party.

But the real reason has his face hidden beneath a beard made of white cotton wool. The beard Paul gave me is far more spectacular than his Father Christmas one. Although Paul has made his Father Christmas look more bizarre by adding dark glasses and a plastic nose. Not surprisingly there's a small crowd round him.

Some boys will totally ignore you when they meet their mates. But Paul hovers over me like a super-efficient waiter, continually filling my glass and making certain all the trays of good food come my way. And I've lost count of how often he's asked me if I'm having a good time.

Paul also brings Dean over. Dean's in black again though Paul's wearing a blue cardigan and white T-shirt which really suit him. And although I'm not prejudiced against Gothics or anything, I'm glad Paul isn't a total Gothic. (He told me later he just likes some of their music.) Dean hasn't bothered with a beard and has just plastered grease-paint over his face. He nods in my direction but isn't exactly friendly. I guess he resents my presence here. Well, I understand that. It is pretty iffy when your best mate gets serious with someone. You're pleased for them of course, but you also feel a bit redundant. And actually, Vicky was slightly strange with me about this party.

'You must really like him,' she said, 'because you won't know a single person there.'

And Vicky wasn't being snidey – she's not that sort of person – she was just amazed at how things were moving so quickly.

In fact, they're moving even faster than Vicky realises. For I'm even thinking of getting serious with Paul, some-one I've known for precisely one day – that's far too soon, isn't it? So how long *does* it take to know someone? Months, I suppose – years, even. But aren't there special times when the whole process speeds up and isn't this one of those times?

We leave around midnight with the party in its beard-swopping phase now. Outside I remove the beard, gulping in a few helpings of air as I do so. I hope I'm not sweating.

'That was great. Thanks a lot.' I hand the beard back to Paul. He's already stashed his disguise in his carrier bag.

'You can have it if you like,' he says unexpectedly.

'Oh no, I couldn't.'

'Yes, go on.'

'But it's expensive – and everyone admired it.'

'So?'

'No, I couldn't.'

He thrusts the beard into my hand – 'I want you to have it.'

'Well, thank you very much.'

Then he lets out one of his sudden bursts of laughter.

'Bet there aren't many boys who give you a beard on a first date.'

'You're definitely the first.'

'I wish I was.'

He squeezes my hand – a kiss is imminent. And it happens so quickly, so smoothly, it's over before I can really enjoy it. I breathe in, a tiny part of his aftershave clings to me.

'Do you want to come back to my house for coffee?' I ask.

'Sure. But won't your parents mind?'

'Probably. I'm already late though, so who cares?'

And I really don't care. I don't quite know why but things I worried about, like my parents going on at me, seem suddenly trivial and unimportant.

'They'll be all right provided we don't wake the twins

10

up. We'll go straight up to my attic. Anyway, Mum likes boys. So when we arrive be ready for my mum going, "And who are you?" and giggling. When friends come round she often starts messing about and telling them stories of what happened to her when she was a girl.'

'She sounds a riot.'

'She is.'

'And what about your dad? Does he do Beastie Boy impressions or . . .?'

'No, he'll just go and hide. He doesn't want to know.'

Yet it's Dad who opens the door. I quickly introduce Paul to him. I know Dad will save any moans until after Paul has gone (and by which time I can pretend to be asleep).

Dad does say: 'Your mother went up to bed some time ago now,' which decoded means – 'It's too late for visitors.' Then I see Dad give Paul's ears a quick appraisal. My dad does not like guys who wear earrings. In fact, he makes them take their earrings out before they cross the family threshold. But Paul isn't wearing any earrings.

My dad beams at him: 'What's the matter with you? You look normal.'

This is the highest compliment Dad can pay anyone. Luckily he can't see into Paul's carrier bag – and he doesn't notice that I'm carrying an orange beard, until I go upstairs. I stifle a giggle but Paul is confused.

'What did your dad mean about me being normal?'

'It means he likes you. And you're not like one of my freaky boyfriends with Mohicans and chains . . .'

'How many boyfriends have you had? Sounds like hundreds.'

I give a mirthless laugh while I warm myself on this sudden blaze of jealousy before saying, 'No, I haven't had many boyfriends. None that matter, anyhow.'

The atmosphere relaxes and Paul gets mighty enthusiastic about my attic. I'm pretty keen on it myself. I was only given it recently as a kind of consolation prize. You see, when the twins were born I was evicted from my large, deluxe bedroom into a freezing rabbit hutch and they said it would only be temporary – that was nearly ten years ago! Anyway, a few globules of guilt must have finally penetrated their conscience: in the New Year they cleared this attic out for me so that I'd have somewhere to entertain my friends. There are actually two rooms – with my main 'entertaining' room leading off to my bedroom – which of course is definitely not for entertaining.

Paul prowls round my attic, while I say apologetically, 'I still haven't totally sorted it out. I'm afraid the furniture belongs in a museum but it's all . . .'

'No, it gives the place atmosphere. I like it.'

'And I don't know why they insisted on white walls. Well, I do – no imagination.'

Paul considers this. 'What you want are more posters. You want to fill every centimetre with them. You could even have some on the ceiling.'

'Wouldn't that make it rather dark?'

'All the better. No, I can probably bring some over.'

A shiver of excitement passes through me. Why, he's acting as if he's looking over a future extension, almost as if he's going to move in here.

'Can I take a peek at your bedroom?' he asks.

'Sure. It's strictly dolls' house size,' I say, opening the door.

'Dead cute, though,' he says. As he walks round my bedroom, I hear my heart pounding away – almost of its own accord and I'm so lost in thought I don't hear what he's saying.

'Caro?'

'Oh, sorry.'

'I was saying I like that little window above your bed. It looks like a porthole.'

'And when it rains it drips condensation on my face. Wonderful.'

Paul takes my hand. 'Come on, you can't fool me. You love this attic don't you?'

I nod almost guiltily.

'And I do too,' he says. 'In fact, I really envy you.'

Still standing inside my bedroom we kind of flow closer together. Another kiss is imminent and no need to rush this one.

'I did knock but I don't think anyone heard me.'

We both jump sheepishly. Mum, sporting her flowered dressing gown, is bearing down on us, eyes brimming with curiosity.

'Mum, this is Paul – Paul, meet my mum.'

As Paul stands up – Mum gives a little tremor of pleasure. I know she's thinking: 'at last Caro's found a nice, well-mannered boy.'

And Mum can barely contain her excitement when she discovers Paul is planning to do 'A' levels – good manners and a future too. From that point Mum goes right over the top and stays there.

'Now then, Paul,' she gushes over him, 'I'm sure you'd like a cup of tea.'

'It's all right, Mum,' I say, 'I'm going to make one up here.'

'Nonsense. Paul wants tea out of a china cup – not out of one of your dirty mugs, don't you, Paul?'

Paul wisely just nods at the irresistible force now hustling downstairs.

'She's only doing this,' I explain, 'so she can keep popping in to check we're not lying on my bed together.'

I mean it as a joke but as I say it a flare of longing passes

13

between us. One day – and I think we'll need at least a day – we will make love. Over and over.

But not when we've any chance of being interrupted by: 'Biscuits, silly me. I forgot the biscuits.' – 'Just checking everything's all right.' – 'Mind if I take the tray now?'

That last time Mum picks the tray up, but then proceeds to lower it again while sneaking her way over to the wicker chair. It is the only decisive action on my part – I open the door for her – that prevents Mum joining us for the rest of the evening.

Before Mum's next entrance which I reckon will be – 'Did you call?' or 'Sorry I thought you called me,' – I switch off the lights.

'This is just a precautionary measure,' I say. 'So we don't get my mum yarning away about her life. But anyhow, you like the dark, don't you?'

'Love it. The dark's brilliant.'

'So just what is it about the dark you like so much?' I ask.

At first we sit a little self-consciously apart on my couch, but the space quickly closes between us. And now Paul's hand curls over my shoulder as if we're in the back row of the cinema, while he says:

'I like the dark because in the dark everything's different, everything takes on a different shape. For instance, you might hang your clothes over your chair and then wake up in the night to find they've turned into a person who's sitting watching you. And though you know it's really still your clothes you have to switch on the lights just to check . . .'

'Oh yes. I know about that. Like I had this totally boring cupboard, but at night I used to wake up convinced there was someone or something in there. In the end I got so terrified they had to take the cupboard out.'

Even now the memory unsettles me.

14

'And did you ever have to check under your bed just to be completely sure no one was there?'

'I still do,' Paul laughs. 'And I'd never leave a leg hanging out at night just in case a nut-job happened to be passing through my bedroom, 'cause at night anything's possible.'

'But it's all rubbish really isn't it?' I say.

'I don't know,' replies Paul. 'Some mighty strange things happen at night.'

'Like what?'

'Like this guy from my class was asleep one night during a mighty bad storm when this old tree goes flying through his window.'

'Was he hurt?'

'No, just very shocked at discovering half a tree on his bed. I mean, can you imagine waking up next to a tree – that must be pretty grim!'

'But that tree story could have happened at any time. Not just at night.'

Paul puts on a mock spooky voice, 'Don't forget though, the dead walk at night. You ask Dean.'

'Why Dean?'

'Well, he collects stories like that.'

'Collects them?'

'Yeah, he writes them down. Got exercise books full of ghost stories.'

I think Dean looks a bit ghostly himself – with his black clothes and very pale, white skin. A ghost with glasses, that's Dean. And I could easily imagine Dean being keen on ghost stories. Still, I don't want to talk about Dean. I want to talk about . . .

'But not all strange things happen in the dead of night,' I say slowly. 'Like yesterday evening, there you were, minding your own business at the Battle of the Bands competition when this girl suddenly starts staring at you. What did you think of me then?'

I sense him hesitating.

'Go on, the truth. I can take it,' I say.

'Cor!'

'What?'

'I thought – cor, my luck's in tonight.'

I can't hide the pleasure his words give me. For when you're tall, lanky and ginger-haired you're not exactly overloaded with compliments. I tend to grow on people. Boys generally ask me to dance after they've known me a couple of months!

But Paul – Paul knew me right away.

I shamelessly fish for more compliments. 'What else did you think last night?'

'To be honest, I wasn't thinking straight at all. I mean, I'd never normally go up to a girl and without a word lead her into a dance. But then I've never gone out with a redhead before.'

I'm not sure if this is a compliment or not. 'So what made you change the habits of a lifetime?'

'Well, last night was like . . . like something flew out of you and touched me.'

The darkness somehow magnifies Paul's words, making them echo in my mind. And I know I'll never forget the way Paul said that. Never! Even though Paul is now squirming beside me going, 'See what the dark does, makes you say things you'd never say normally. I must have read that somewhere . . .'

On Monday after school I arrive home to find a small, thin box waiting for me – and Mum and my twin sisters, Andrea and Nicky, clustering round it.

'Arrived just as we got in,' says Mum. 'There is a card,' she adds.

I open the card. It reads, 'Caro – Love Ya. Paul'.

'Love Ya,' reads Mum over my shoulders. 'Love Ya,' she repeats the phrase as if trying to translate it.

But I'm already opening the box. Inside is a single, deep-red rose.

There's much 'oohing' and 'aahing' as the twins are allowed to place it in a vase, and slowly and ceremoniously take it up to my attic. A trail of petals follow them. And the rose continues to spill when it is situated in the position of honour, beneath my spotlight.

By the time Paul rings, the rose is hanging over the vase and fading fast. I stare at the rose, willing it to hang on until tomorrow night when Paul comes round. But next day I wake up to find the rose hunched on the side of my vase with what look like black thumb prints creeping over its remaining petals. I cannot bear looking at such a sickly specimen – and I know neither could Paul. So I ask Mum to bury my rose in the bin. But unknown to me, Mum rings up the florist and complains. She is an excellent complainer. And waiting for me that afternoon is another box.

'You can pretend this is Paul's rose,' says Mum eagerly.

When I was young, Mum used to love repairing my toys, she was forever sewing on a new ear for Teddy. Now she's repairing Paul's presents.

I open the box and for a second – just a second, the light goes out of Mum's eyes.

For the rose is white.

And white roses are a bad omen, aren't they? It was Mum who told me. They symbolise – I can't remember exactly – but something bad. Now though, Mum pretends not to remember.

'It's just red roses are more appropriate than white ones because they symbolise love. I'm going to have a few words to say to that flower shop.'

'No don't, Mum. Please don't. Just tell me what white roses symbolise.'

'Nothing. Absolutely nothing,' says Mum quickly. But I keep remembering the way that look of fear shot across her face like a sudden charge of lightning. Only I'm too scared to press her. I don't want to know what bad thing is waiting out there for me.

The white rose gleams, glistens and smirks in the lounge, taunting me with its secrets. Until I can bear it no longer.

So now, in the bin there's a silky white rose in full bloom – while somewhere beneath it my red rose decays into dust.

Two Months Later

'What exactly have I got to do with Dean tonight?'

It's Friday afternoon and Vicky and I, both still in our school uniform, are sprawled over the couch in my attic.

'Well, you haven't got to make mad passionate love to him,' I reply.

'I'll leave that to you and Paul, shall I?' says Vicky, smiling sweetly.

I throw a cushion at her before continuing. 'All you've got to do is be your nice, friendly self by smiling at Dean a lot and generally, cheering him up.'

'So just why did she chuck him?'

'Don't really know. I mean, I hardly knew her. Paul'd been trying to fix Dean up for ages. Then at this party there was a girl who was into the same freak music as Dean and it seemed they were made for each other. But after two weeks she chucked him – and has got a new boyfriend already.'

'Poor Dean,' says Vicky. 'He'll probably spend the evening sobbing into his beer. Inviting him here tonight was Paul's idea, I suppose.'

'It was mine, actually.'

'Really!' Vicky is incredulous. 'Yet you and Dean don't exactly get on, do you?'

'No, not at all. But for one crazy moment I felt sorry

for him and thought how sad that Paul's best mate has never been up here.'

'Caro – you've got a heart of sheer mush,' says Vicky.

'Now, though, I wish like anything I'd never told Paul he could invite Dean round – tonight of all nights.'

'Of course,' says Vicky, 'there couldn't be a worse time, for this is your last night with Paul.'

'Don't put it like that or you'll have me blubbering.'

'All right, your last night with Paul for an entire two weeks.' Vicky's tone becomes mocking. 'And for you both that will seem an eternity, won't it?' She clasps her hand to her brow. 'It's all so tragic. Paul forced to go to Cornwall with his parents, leaving you . . .'

'All right, Sarky.'

'But I mean it,' says Vicky in a voice dripping with sarcasm. 'For this means Caro might even be forced to – horror of horrors – spend time with her best friend again,' Vicky pauses, timing her last shot, 'after all this time.'

I sit up. 'Are you trying to make me feel guilty?'

'Yes.'

'Well, you're succeeding.'

'Good.' Vicky's smiling, but not on the inside, if you know what I mean.

My smile back is just plain uneasy. I hate it when people say things as a joke, but also mean something.

Vicky suddenly sighs nostalgically. 'I used to practically live up here, do you remember? It was just after you got the attic – your mum caught me smoking up here.'

'Oh yes, what was it she said to you?'

'She said, "Vicky, if you smoke now, when you have a child, it will be born smaller than the rest, you know".' We both laugh.

'Oh, your mum cracks me up. And your little sisters . . .'

We're both digging up funny incidents now.

'What about when I borrowed your ski pants,' recalls Vicky, 'and sat in a pot of cold cream. You were so mad.'

'Oh, I wasn't!'

'You were. In fact you stayed mad until you needed me to ring up – who was it?'

I shake my head.

'Oh, come on you must remember, some guy you were mad about one day – and couldn't stand the next.'

'Who knows?' I say vaguely. 'It could be anyone. I was always going off boys then.'

'Some of us still are,' says Vicky, adding quietly: 'It seems ages ago now, doesn't it? And even though it isn't very far away, our past seems to be rushing away from us.'

There's a rather uncomfortable silence broken by Vicky getting up and exclaiming: 'This attic's really improved, there's a real buzz up here now. And I love all those pictures on the ceiling.' She turns her head and squints, 'He's quite nice-looking. Who is he?'

'Larry Mullen Jr from U2.'

Vicky smiles. 'You wouldn't have known that two months ago – and all these records – Paul's everywhere in this attic now, isn't he . . . ? Well, remember if it hadn't been for me, you and Paul might never have met. I still can't believe how you both met and became everything to each other in the space of about four seconds – why, that's frightening. No, not frightening. Why did I say that?'

Vicky laughs nervously. 'And why am I pacing about your room and gabbling on as if I'm talking to a stranger – not my best friend since Fish-Eyes' class, ten years ago. I think I'd better sit down.'

'Vicky . . .' I begin.

'No, no, let me just ask you one question. Please.'

'Sure.'

Her voice softens. 'What's it like, Caro?'

'What do you mean?'

'You know. You and Paul and all this True Love stuff.'

I instantly turn away from her but she squeezes my hand.

'No, honestly, I want to know. You read about true love in magazines every week but what's it really like?'

There's no trace of sarcasm in her voice now and her eyes stare at me dreamily as if I'm about to describe a faraway place she's never visited.

I let out a slow, deep breath. 'You know Bug.'

'Bug, the chemistry teacher?'

'Yes. Do you remember him talking about his flying exploits?'

'I remember him talking, but I don't remember listening.'

'Well there was one thing he said that I do remember.'

'About love?'

'No, no.' I smile at the thought of Bug talking to us about love. 'Just hang on a second.'

'Sorry. I won't interrupt again.'

'Well, Bug said that when you go up in an aeroplane the world below gets very small – that's obvious. But when you get up really high, like up to 25,000 feet, something else happens. The air's different, everything's different, and it's as if you've journeyed into another dimension. Well, that's how it's been for me since I met Paul. I feel as if I've jumped into another dimension and all the things I used to do have shrunk. When I think of them now – it's as if I'm looking at them through the wrong end of a telescope.'

Vicky stands up. 'I'm not listening to any more because you're making me so jealous. I'm jealous but I'm also excited for you. Does that make sense? And I'm happy too, because Paul's a good laugh and, now you've smartened him up, very good-looking, especially in that blue-checked jacket which I bet you picked out. And as for you – you're looking great, like a red-haired Marilyn Monroe.'

22

'Come on, Vicky, you're the Marilyn Monroe look-alike, but thanks.'

And all at once we're hugging each other.

'We'll always be friends,' I tell Vicky. 'Always.'

And Vicky goes, 'You've made my mascara run now, saying that.' She smiles and says – 'Don't worry, I'll keep an eye on Dean tonight.'

'Well, if all else fails,' I say, 'and the evening's going really badly, Paul's going to switch off the lights and say, "Dean, why don't you tell us a ghost story?"'

II

At nine o'clock Paul switches off the lights and says, 'Dean, why don't you tell us a ghost story?'

I heave a sigh of relief. It's been a terrible evening. Dean has just sat there in an awful white shirt covered in what looks like flicked red ink, his face stiff with tension. And he never relaxes. Just keeps talking in a low whisper to Paul about music, while practically ignoring poor Vicky. Not to mention me.

I try to be understanding. Perhaps he's so cut up about being chucked he hates all females. Yet surely he could at least try and talk to us. And I can't help resenting Dean, and the way he's wrecking my last night with Paul. And to think this was all my idea!

Still, at least in the dark I can relax on the couch with Paul. I lie back, letting the scent of Paul's aftershave lap over me, as if I'm luxuriating in a bath.

'Dean's a wicked story-teller,' Paul whispers to me, then turns to Dean, 'Okay, Dean – action.'

A low, toneless newsreader voice threads its way through the darkness: 'You probably know that Norsfield School – that's Paul's and my school – is well over a hundred years old. There's this caretaker, Mr Gochin . . .'

'Who's also well over a hundred years old,' interrupts Paul.

'He's certainly old,' says Dean. 'And he's quite frail and doddery now.'

'But he can still grab a boy's shoulder where it really hurts,' says Paul.

'Well, you're the bad lad, not me,' says Dean. 'Anyway, every year Gochin takes the second-years out for a ghost hunt and when Paul and I were second-years we went. At eight o'clock we're all waiting outside St Bede's Church chattering away, when Gochin slowly ambles towards us, leaning heavily on this old stick. Then he raises this stick in the air commanding us all to be silent and makes us stand there in silence for several minutes before he gives us a run-down on all the ghosts that lurk around us. By now we're getting more and more psyched up. Then he tells us about the school's first caretaker and how he had his head cut off.'

'Eeer!' I cry.

Paul squeezes my hand. At once I'm ashamed of myself but I let him go on holding my hand.

'I think he lost his head doing some sort of maintenance work,' says Dean vaguely. 'But his wife, according to several eye-witness accounts, is still there, wandering round the school at night, searching for her headless husband.

'Anyway, after telling us this, Gochin holds up some keys. "Here are the keys to my room," he says. "I never leave anything in my room at night because of her. But tonight I left a matchbox on my worktable – it's the only thing on the table – so you can't miss it. All I want is for one volunteer to go and fetch it for me." It's a simple request. But for ages we all stand there, studying the patterns on our shoes. No one dares go in there. Until this one guy – Terry Wilson – volunteers.

24

'After Terry's gone, Gochin stands waiting for him, with a really funny look on his face as if he knows something we don't.'

Dean's voice slowly rises.

'Terry's gone for ages, and Gochin looks more and more creepy. Just as we're wondering if Terry will ever return he stumbles towards us, white as a sheet and unable to speak. "Leave him," commands Gochin straight away. "He's had a nasty shock." And Gochin leads Terry away from us and in front of the church. Finally Terry, still moving unsteadily, joins us again and tells us what happened.

'Terry'd gone towards our school, actually feeling quite confident as he took in the familiar surroundings. He'd opened the caretaker's door, was unable to find the light switch but still located the matchbox right away. The room felt icy cold and Terry got ready to make a hasty exit with the matchbox, when he heard a woman's voice . . . She was calling his name. For a moment Terry's whole body went into that kind of paralysis you get in nightmares but then he heard her call again in a deep mournful voice, "Terry, Terry!" and he shot out of there faster than the speed of light. Of course he forgot all about the matchbox. Later Terry asked Gochin how the ghost knew his name. And Gochin smiled. "She wasn't calling you. You see, her husband's name was Terry, perhaps she mistook you for him." He added, "If it's any consolation to you, I've done this ghost hunt for years and years and no one has yet managed to remove the matchbox."'

Dean's story ends with a burst of enthusiastic applause. Despite myself I'm impressed. He's a lousy guest – but a great story-teller. And while he was talking I found myself picturing him – with his deathly white skin and gloomy black clothes – and wondering what went on inside his head.

But then Vicky says, 'I thought you were going to tell the other ghost story, Dean. The one about the matron who was hacked to bits while she was taking a bath.'

Dean replies, 'I didn't think I'd better tell anything too scary because I know how easily girls get uptight.'

'Sexist rubbish,' cry Vicky and I in angry chorus.

'Now, come on, Caroline, you were scared, in fact you were wetting yourself during my story, wasn't she, Paul?' says Dean.

I bristle furiously. Just as I was weakening towards him, he taunts me like this. And why is he picking on me?

Paul doesn't agree with Dean – but he doesn't argue either – just laughs.

'I wasn't scared at all by your story, Dean,' I say through clenched teeth.

'I think you were.' Dean's voice is disbelieving and smug.

How dare he try and ridicule me – especially after I've tried so hard to be nice to him. How dare he! And all at once something breaks inside me.

'In my opinion – your story wasn't really a ghost story at all.' I'm talking wildly, surprising even myself by what I'm saying.

'It's easy to see what really happened. That mad old caretaker gets you well and truly spooked up, probably fuses the lights in his room and lets your schoolboy imagination do the rest. So it's obvious to me – you were conned.'

If I could see Dean I'd probably stop now but the darkness spurs me on somehow. I press home my advantage.

'And you notice it's only the little kids he takes on ghost hunts. The older ones wouldn't fall for such little tricks and stories. Besides, any mature person knows that ghosts don't really exist.'

'Oh yes they do.' Dean's voice is low, but there's no mistaking the suppressed fury behind his words.

'You believe in life after death then?' I ask him.

'Certainly. It's life before death I'm not sure I believe in.'

'Is that supposed to be clever?' I say jeeringly.

'They say there's a ghost in McDonalds,' puts in Vicky suddenly, 'down in the stock room. People keep hearing boxes being knocked down when there's no one there. And last week (so Mark Edmunds told me) they were supposed to sort out the new stock – but no one could be bothered. Then at five o'clock they all go down there, thinking they'd better make a start and find it's all been done. Someone had neatly packed all the stock away – a job that takes ages – yet no one had gone near the stock room all day!'

'My, what a nice, helpful ghost,' I say.

'Perhaps we can get one for up here?' Paul laughs faintly, I feel his warm breath on my neck.

Across from us, Dean isn't laughing or moving. I picture him stiff and rigid with anger – as I conclude:

'That McDonalds story just proves how silly all this talk of ghosts existing is.'

For a moment there is silence. Has Dean conceded defeat? But then . . .

'Now listen well, Caroline, while I explain something to you. Energy can never be created or destroyed. It just changes from one form into another. That's all physical death means. Our body stops but our energy carries on – that's what your soul is – a force of energy.'

'So where do all these forces of energy go?' I ask.

'They take up residence in the astral form.'

'The what? No, I'm sorry, Dean, that's just a lot of waffly mumbo-jumbo strictly for sad old ladies.'

'I think that's something of a generalisation, Caroline.'

27

His pompous tone inflames me all over again. 'No it isn't. There's absolutely no proof for what you say.'

'There's plenty of proof. Hundreds of eye-witness accounts, for one.'

'But no scientific proof?'

'Science is not capable of explaining everything. But I know ghosts exist.'

'How do you know?'

'Because I have a great-aunt who's psychic. You should talk to her.'

'Look, if she's happy believing what she believes, that's fine. But don't expect me to believe it.'

'You won't let yourself believe it,' says Dean. 'But anyway I have proof.' He pauses, 'I have seen a ghost.'

For a moment there is no sound except for the dull rustle of the wind outside.

'You have seen a ghost?' I know my voice is shrinking.

'You never told me that, mate,' says Paul.

Again all interest and attention is on Dean. But this time he doesn't seem to welcome it. His voice sounds muffled and even smaller than mine.

'Last year I saw a ghost – the ghost of my dog.'

'Your dog.' I seize on this, exclaiming scornfully – 'Now I've heard everything. What about budgies and goldfish and hamsters – seen any ghosts of them?'

Dean's shadow jerks into life, and stumbles towards the door. I sit trembling, not quite understanding why we're both getting so worked up. But before Dean can leave Paul stands up, rushing his 'Life is a party', voice into the atmosphere.

'Hey, wouldn't it be great being a ghost – for a day or two at any rate? You know what I'd do – I'd go and poke all the people in the eye who've given me grief. Magic. How about you, Vick?' he appeals to the other neutral observer. 'Oh sorry, you hate being called Vick – really gets up your nose, doesn't it?' (Most of Paul's jokes are as bad as that.)

'It's the floating I'd like. I'd float round the world, I think,' muses Vicky.

'Yeah, just think of it,' Paul goes on. 'Floating right up there, with the sky close enough to touch. That must be a brilliant sensation. I remember . . .' He pauses, then adds, his voice shaking with excitement. 'But of course, why don't we do it now? It'll be great, won't it?'

'What will?' I ask curiously.

'Some levitation, that's what,' cries Paul, darting into the centre of the room and falling on to the ground.

'Remember, Dean, when we did this round Roly's house?' he calls upwards.

'You need more people,' says Dean, 'got to have at least five.' But he's edging away from the door – towards Paul. We all are.

'Nah, we can do it with three if we concentrate really hard. And we've got the right conditions – dark, talk of ghosts – couldn't be better. You'll do it, won't you, girls?'

Paul's managing to nudge events his way and we're all circling round him now, Dean and I taking care to keep far apart.

'What have we got to do, then?' asks Vicky.

Paul writhes round on the floor. 'I don't do anything except lie here while you concentrate so hard your thoughts beam me up, up, and away.'

'It'll never work,' I say.

'Don't you want to do it then, Caroline?' says Dean.

'I didn't say that,' I reply quickly.

I hate the thought of Dean directing operations, but Paul's so keen about this . . . Besides, it's bound to be a flop.

'If Paul wants to, we'll do it, won't we, Vicky?'

29

'Oh yes. I've always wanted to do this anyhow,' says Vicky.

'Right then.' Dean resumes his favourite role – as local guru. 'What we do firstly is: Vicky, you stand there,' he points to Paul's thigh, 'Caroline, you go by his feet, and I shall stand here.'

Dean has of course positioned himself at the head.

Gazing down at Paul, it's strange how his face shows up so much lighter and clearer than anyone else's. It's as if all the stray glints of light are converging round him, displaying his perfect complexion – Paul's one of the few guys who hasn't even got one spot. He looks up at me and winks. He's all excited, just like a little kid.

'Right, come on, Paul, you have to relax completely,' orders Dean.

He then directs me to hold Paul's ankles while his hands are just under Paul's shoulders. Vicky flutters rather uncertainly round Paul's thigh. This is never going to work.

'Before I ask you to lift Paul up, close your eyes – you too, Paul – and concentrate. Think of Paul floating upwards.'

Fourteen seconds of concentration – then I get the giggles.

'What's wrong?' snaps Dean.

'Your breathing's doing me in. Can't you breathe more quietly?'

'You don't want to do this, do you?' says Dean, all snidey.

'Yes, I do but . . .'

'Come on, Caro, give it a go!' calls Paul.

'I am. I have been concentrating, it's just I can't take all Dean's heavy breathing.'

'Well, if Dean breathes more quietly we'll begin again,' says Vicky calmly.

'My breathing is perfectly normal,' mutters Dean.

We start again. This time no one laughs.

'Now keep your eyes closed and repeat everything I say,' instructs Dean. 'This boy looks very tired.'

'This boy looks very tired,' chant Vicky and I.

'This boy is growing weak.'

'This boy is fading now.'

Echoing the words makes them linger and grow. I shiver.

'This boy has gone away,' the whole room seems to shudder and gasp.

'This boy is weightless.'

'Now push,' whispers Dean.

And we're lifting Paul so easily. Really easily. He's so light, it's almost as if he is weightless, as if he has . . . I lose concentration. So does Vicky. Paul's full weight returns to my mind – and hands. He thuds back to earth, waving an arm right in Dean's face.

'Hey, watch it,' exclaims Dean.

'Sorry, mate,' cries Paul. 'But I was going right out of control.'

He's all flushed.

'How far did I go?'

'Only a few inches,' said Dean, 'then the girls lost concentration.'

'But it felt like much more. And when you started to drop me it was as if I was dropping miles. Some mates did that to me once: they put their hands underneath this chair I was sitting on. I started going right up until something touched my head. Then I was really shedding my load because I thought I'd hit the ceiling. Turns out, they'd put this plank of wood on my head – and I'd gone up about six inches. Still, it's a totally brilliant feeling.'

'We can get you up much higher,' says Dean, 'if everyone concentrates,' he adds.

'Come on then,' says Paul. 'I want to go right up there this time.'

There's no refusing Paul, of course. And this time he ascends quite a lot higher – and after he drops to the ground he's gabbling away so excitedly, you'd think he'd just come off a rollercoaster or something.

I'm not enjoying this game, though. I don't like the words Dean uses and I hate the way Paul's weight just dissolves away to nothing. It makes me feel uneasy.

So before Paul can ask to go up again I disappear down to the loo, switching the lights on before I go. I'm keeping those lights on for the rest of the evening too. But when I return I'm blinking in bewilderment. The attic's gone dark again – and silent. And my eyes will have to get used to the dark again before I can see anything. What a nuisance and . . . where are they? I call out.

'Come on. Switch on the lights.'

Not a sound penetrates the thick blackness, until I hear a whisper from somewhere high, high above me. I hear the voice again. It's Paul. Only his voice seems to be floating off the highest part of the ceiling, as if he . . . It's just Paul being silly. I know that. But it's as if I also know something else, something bad, for dark forces are gathering round me. And a picture's forming but I don't want to see it. I won't see it. A shiver slices through me and I shudder, swaying backwards as the room blurs and fades away. I never actually pass out, yet I come close, standing right on the border. But I manage to keep dimly aware of the three pairs of hands anxiously clamouring round me and oh so gently depositing me in the wicker chair. Then I hear Paul say, 'We must do something,' and he sounds so concerned a smile creeps across my lips.

'I'm all right,' I gasp.

But I'm not all right. You know when people talk about the cold going right through them and it taking ages for them to thaw out – well, that's how I'm feeling. It's as if the terror had gone right through me, boring itself into my bloodstream. And every so often I start shaking again as fresh bursts of panic tear through me.

And then suddenly it's over. Like a gale that has blown itself out. I'm feeling a bit shaky, but that's all. The room comes into focus again and I bend down and pick up Teddy – who was shoved out of his wicker chair to make way for me – and sit patting him, feeling a little wobbly and more than a little absurd.

Paul gives me a hug, while Vicky is full of apologies and Dean cringes in the corner. The little joke had been his idea. Paul had climbed on to Dean's back, stood high up near the ceiling and called out to me in the darkness.

'We thought you'd laugh,' says Paul. 'Didn't you recognise my voice?'

It's easier to lie. 'No,' I reply. 'I didn't.'

'It was probably your unconcious taking control,' says Dean. 'In your unconscious you do believe in ghosts.'

But he didn't dare pursue the point. I almost wished he was right. Perhaps he was. It's only ... Why was I so terrified when I recognised Paul's voice? I shiver, best to forget it, just a joke that went wrong. My fault, really – I over-reacted. Now there's nothing left of the evening except embarrassment.

'I think I'd better go,' says Vicky.

Everyone decides to go.

I see Dean and Vicky off – Vicky's still apologising while Dean keeps giving me these odd glances as if he's a detective who doesn't quite believe a suspect's story. I'm not sorry to see him go. Now at last Paul and I can have a few minutes together. But before I even close the door ...

'Paul, why have you always got your arm round my sister?' Twin One – Andrea – is peering down the staircase and smiling flirtatiously. She's got a crush on Paul (amongst many others). So has Niki, Twin Two – but she's rather more reserved about expressing her devotion. She just stares solemnly at us, a thumb stuck in her mouth.

'Yo – Andrea. Yo – Niki,' yells Paul.

As he hasn't any sisters of his own, he rather over-rates my little jabbermouths.

'Don't encourage them,' I whisper. 'Or we'll never get rid of them.'

But it's too late.

'I've seen you kissing my sister,' giggles Andrea and adds, while pulling at her yellow nightie. 'I wore a bra today, Paul.'

'Cor,' says Paul, winking at her.

Their giggles become louder and high-pitched but quickly fall away when they see Mum charging out of the lounge.

'Get to sleep now,' she roars, without even looking up at them.

'Paul spoke to us first,' says Andrea promptly.

'Goodnight, Paul,' she adds sweetly.

Paul and I hover uncertainly as Mum moans on, 'They were asleep ten minutes ago!'

'We were only saying goodnight,' I reply.

I'm always getting blamed if they do anything wrong. But Mum won't be angry for long if Paul's around. When I told Paul that my parents think he's 'very sensible', he wasn't exactly flattered. But that's their highest compliment. Mum's even limiting her checks on us to twenty a night now!

'Looking forward to your holiday then, Paul?' asks Mum.

'No, not really.' Paul smiles almost apologetically.

'Still, I've no doubt you'll enjoy it when you get there. And we'll look forward to hearing all about it when you get back.'

Before turning upstairs she adds, 'I expect you'll need a good night's sleep too.'

'She's not exactly subtle, is she?' I say.

'No, but she's right. I'd better go. We're leaving at four o'clock tomorrow morning.' He frowns. 'Two weeks with my folks – pretty pukey. Still, I'll be out on my boat every day, leaving them far behind.'

'Wish I could leave mine far behind,' I say.

As if on cue, Mum begins her twin-screeching.

'Are you gonna miss me then?' I ask.

'Nah, glad to be rid of you.'

'Same here. Soon as you've gone I'm going to fill that attic with blokes.'

'Starting with Dean tomorrow,' he teases.

'That boy is . . .'

'He's okay when you get to know him. Most people are really.'

'I think they should settle now if there are no more disturbances,' proclaims Mum, pounding back downstairs.

'I'm just off,' says Paul quickly.

'Well, have a nice time, dear,' she says. 'We'll miss you.'

We wait for her to retreat back to the sitting room. But instead, she stands at the bottom of the stairs, twin-listening.

So I put the door on the latch and we both step outside, but not before –

'Don't stay out there long without a coat on. There's quite a chill tonight.'

'Give me strength,' I mutter.

Paul clutches my hand. I gaze at his long narrow fingers and the clumps of black hair on his knuckles. And then I'm lost in his kiss, his embrace. I'm happy and warm and safe until he finally starts to leave.

'You sure you're okay now?' he asks.

I nod. I'm okay; except for this awful ache and emptiness inside me every time I think of him going away.

'And look after yourself, won't you?' he says, looking right at me and smiling.

No one sees me as Paul does. The best of me lives only in his eyes.

'Next time you see me I'll have a really husky suntan,' says Paul, still smiling determinedly. He goes to put on his Walkman, begins his loose-rolling walk, then stops: 'Nearly forgot. I did this for you. It's not as good as I wanted it to be . . .'

Out of his pocket he produces an envelope.

'A letter already,' I say.

But inside is a small card on which he's drawn a picture of a totally healthy red rose in a vase. It's really detailed and must have taken him hours and hours. 'To make up for the dud rose I gave you,' he says.

'I'd forgotten all about that,' I lie.

It's not until after I've watched him disappear into the darkness I see he's scrawled a message on the back: 'Now you can keep your red rose for ever.'

Part Two – by Caro:
Two Weeks Later

I wake with a start. My neck feels stiff and uncomfortable and for one bleary moment I don't know why I'm sprawled out on the sofa in the sitting room.

If only I can stretch out that moment of ignorance. But my mind's clicked back into place already and there's no way I can stop it rushing back now.

What time is it? Not sure. It must be the afternoon – because I had lunch – or rather I was offered lunch. And it's Saturday because Mum and Niki have gone shopping, leaving . . .

The sitting room door opens very slowly, very gently, quite unlike Andrea's normal entrance. Instantly I snap my eyes shut.

'Caro, do you want a nice cup of tea?' whispers Andrea, in exactly the same tone Mum uses.

I breathe a little heavier, just to make sure she realises I'm asleep – and leaves me alone. But instead she tiptoes over to me and tugs at my blanket which has sunk on to the carpet. Andrea hoists the blanket back over me, managing to temporarily smother me as she does so. She then spends ages smoothing down every corner of the blanket before stealing out again so quietly. I'm not certain for ages if she's still standing in the doorway watching me.

But at last I can open my eyes and hurl the blanket back on the floor. That's the last thing I need. I'm burning up already. It's funny, I've always hated boys who had clammy hands but right now my whole body feels clammy and sweaty, as if I'm running a fever. Yet, I'm not ill and I'm not an invalid – even if my family persist in treating me as one. As if to prove it, I get up, rather unsteadily and stand staring out of the window where the rain is giving the window a pretty intensive battering. In fact, it's beating down with such fury and such hostility, you'd think the rain is trying to smash through the glass. Actually, it's a sight I could really appreciate if only the sky wasn't such a bleached white colour. I want a dark, broody scene – not this unnatural, stinging brightness.

I make as if to draw the curtains but instead, I just flop back on to the sofa again. Perhaps they're right, I have become an invalid. I don't know. I only know I've no energy left. None. Not that I want any energy. Too dangerous. For then I'd start thinking and . . . That's why I daren't go upstairs and instead, lie exiled down here in this kind of limbo where nothing seems real – that's what saves me.

I close my eyes again. I can sleep any time now, night or day. Just like my gran. I used to watch her, one second talking and nodding away, the next, mouth open and fast asleep – and I'd wonder how she did that. How could she just drift away like that? Suddenly, I'm as adept as her at slipping off. I'm doing it now, dwindling away, but something stops me. Someone's whispering. It's Andrea, obviously using Mum's absence to ring a friend and they're talking about me. Only her whisper is more piercing than her normal voice.

'Caro's still really upset,' she says it proudly. 'We're all very worried about her. She loved him very much. She was going to marry Paul, you know . . .' I can't help smiling. Andrea's a born story-teller, she can't resist decorating the facts for more dramatic effect. And yet – one day Paul and I would have married. That is surely true.

'I had my picture taken yesterday by the *Stevenage Express*. And this man said he thought I was much older than nine and that I was looking after my sister really well. I told him she doesn't need much looking after, she's asleep most of the time . . . Yes, this Thursday I should be in. They wanted a picture of . . . What? Yes, he was out all alone in his sailboat. They say it was the boom which hit Paul . . . Yes, boom,' Andrea's reciting now.

'A boom's a piece of wood which is on the bottom of the mast and it swings from side to side and my dad says if you're not paying attention when there's a gust of wind, the boom can get loose, swing round and hit you on the head. And my dad says that's what happened to Paul, 'cause when they found Paul he had this nasty blow on his head . . . Yes, he was . . .'

It's as if that awful word is scratching at her throat and all she can utter is a tiny choking kind of sob. And I know what's happening. Every so often the full horror of what you're saying – or even thinking – creeps up on you all over again. Your mind can't take it in the first time – or the forty-first time – perhaps it can never take it in.

At last Andrea recovers herself by returning to Mum's comforting chant. 'And Paul was such a nice boy, so friendly and open, just like one of the family and he . . .'

I curl up tighter. I don't want to hear any more. And instantly, it's as if a wall of soundproof glass surrounds me. In fact, I think that wall's there pretty permanently. For sounds keep blacking out on me and I float away . . . But hold on, I can hear something. A voice has broken through. It sounds far off, though, so perhaps if I don't answer it'll fade away. But then the voice draws closer. I shoot up. It can't be. It's impossible.

'Paul, is that you?'

'Of course it's me.'

The light flashes on and I blink incredulously. For there is Paul, standing in front of me, looking so fresh-faced and real. I can't reply at first. How could I ever have dreamt that he'd . . .

'You okay?' he asks, sitting beside me.

'I've had this horrible dream,' I say.

He smiles. 'Get chased by a big bad bogeyman, did you?'

'No, I dreamt you'd drowned in a boating accident while you were away on holiday. Your sailboat capsized and you . . .'

'No chance,' he interrupts quickly, then grins broadly. 'Don't you know I have a swimming certificate, third place in the twenty-five yards, awarded by my Infants' School and . . .'

I'm still shivering. He clutches my hand.

'That was a pretty heavy dream, wasn't it?'

I can only nod, as tears well up.

'And you missed me, didn't you?' He smiles gently, until all at once I'm enveloped by a rush of aftershave and tenderness as he hugs me tightly. I close my eyes and he's murmuring something in my ear. I giggle . . . what's Paul saying?

'Caro, do you want a nice cup of tea?'

I blink in disbelief, then put up my hands as if to shut out everything in my gaze.

'Caro, are you all right?'

What's going on? Why does Andrea's voice keep prodding at me? Anyone would think I'd just been dreaming. But I haven't. Impossible. For it was so real – I actually felt Paul in my arms. Can still feel him. No, that was no dream – dreams are misty, confusing, incomprehensible things. This is my dream now, isn't it? Only I feel a bit muddled as if I'm reading two stories alternately. Yes, this is definitely the dream, for it's so silly. I mean, Mum and Niki have joined Andrea now and they're all arranging themselves round me. Look at Niki in her little leather coat – new, I think – and Mum in her brown and yellow check coat. Only Dad's missing. Perhaps I'll dream him up in a minute.

Only I'd rather wake up now. Please. Oh Paul – where are you? Help me. They're all talking at me again and Mum's placing her hand on my forehead.

What's she saying?

'Did you have another nightmare?'

I shake my head but I don't answer. How can I explain this is the nightmare.

'Would you like a nice cup of tea?' asks Mum.

That question again. I don't even like tea much but I say, 'Yes please.'

Great sighs of relief all round. Andrea and Niki already skipping eagerly towards the door.

'Put a teabag in for your dad too,' says Mum. 'He should be home any minute now. And remember to let the tea brew this time.'

Then Mum kneels down beside me. I can't help noticing her fearsome blue tights.

'Are you feeling any better?'

It's about then I know I'm in what they call reality. It's the sheer drabness, sheer ordinariness of it all that makes me realise this is no dream. For I could never dream anything as dull and hopeless and two-dimensional as this.

'Are you feeling any better, dear?' Mum repeats her question, only this time there's a definite crack of anxiety in her voice. The room is deathly silent, save for the sound of the rain keeping up its assault – until I reply –

'Yes, I feel a bit better.'

My usual ritual answer – how can I explain what I really feel – that most of the time I either feel numb and woozy or so full of rage and fury I'm sure I will explode. At times I hate everyone. Even Paul. How could he just go and leave me here, isolated, stranded, totally alone.

'I saw Paul's mother today,' went on Mum gently. 'She quite understood that you don't feel up to the funeral.'

'But what's the point of going? Paul's not there.'

'And she said if ever you wanted to talk to her . . .'

'Why would I want to talk to her?' I interrupt rudely. 'It's all her fault anyhow.'

'Well, that's a little harsh,' begins Mum gently. 'Anyway, she seems to be bearing up and she said she's had so many letters and phone calls from people all saying what a really nice boy Paul was and . . . Ah, here's tea.'

Andrea begins her stately procession towards me – of course she's filled my cup right up to the brim – and the tea trickles along the carpet. Niki follows with an equally full cup of tea and dribbling even more generous helpings on to the carpet. Yet Mum only says, rather vaguely:

'Get a sponge, dear,' to Niki and then returns to me.

As soon as Dad arrives he's in the doorway staring at me too. And I can really sense their concern. Only no one knows what to say. No one speaks my language.

I sit up to drink my tea and wince. Andrea's plonked my cup right on top of Paul's postcard. I check the card. I don't want any tea stains on it, nothing must taint this card. It's strange really. This card arrived the morning after . . . It was quite late, the evening the phone went and I answered it, thinking it was Vicky and instead it was Paul's dad. And afterwards when I tried to speak and explain to Mum and Dad what had happened I couldn't. It was as if my voice was drowning in a thick black liquid. And anyway, what I was saying was so incomprehensible. How could Paul, who was always so laid back and mellow and – so much more alive than anyone else in the world be . . . If someone had to go why couldn't it have been one of the nasty, useless people – there's so many of them – but not Paul. It's all so senseless, so pointless.

And that night – my first night in the sitting room – I hardly slept at all. And if I did sleep for a moment a sudden surge of pain would wake me up again, as another piece of my heart smashed itself into pieces.

Finally, I got up to go to the loo and be sick when I noticed the post was already on the mat: two bills, a circular, something else in a dull brown envelope – and a card with a very pretty view of the Cornish sea.

Paul can only have been in Cornwall about two minutes before sending it off – as he hadn't even been sailing at that point. Instead, he wrote how he'd be going as far out to sea as he could the next day, and he'd added a smudged doodle of himself in a boat. Above his head he'd put a thought bubble, just one word inside it: CARO. His last words were heavily underlined. SEE YOU VERY SOON.

II

That night I decide it's time to go home. I walk briskly through the attic, not daring to look round, and immediately get ready for bed, even though it's only about eight o'clock. Mum's put Teddy by my pillow – just like she did when I had my tonsils out. For a while I sit up in bed reading – or rather reading the same word over and over. In the end I give up and just lie there, watching the room swell up with darkness as night swallows day. Just like it always does.

I feel wrecked but I can't sleep. It's too noisy – especially my clock, which even when flung on the carpet continues ticking dementedly. The sound goes right through me. I throw a pillow over it. But the tiny, half-muffled tickings are more irritating than before. Finally I hurl two jumpers over it too. Only then is the ticking wiped out – defeated.

43

But another, far worse noise, takes over – strange creaking sounds from just beyond my door. Now hold on, don't panic, these are not strange sounds. All attics creak. It's just loose boards, that's all. And of course, the creakings sound louder at night. Much louder.

Yet, there's another much fainter creaking noise. That doesn't sound like loose boards, rather it's the noise someone makes when sitting down on my old wicker chair. And that noise sounds as if someone's leaning back in my chair. Waiting.

But I'm being absurd, regressing to my infant days when every night I convinced myself that someone was hiding in my room, camouflaged by the impenetrable blackness. And this demon was only waiting until I slept before he would pounce on me, ready to throttle every ounce of life from me: until the morning when I'd be found – with my eyes forever locked into a look of terror.

I shiver. I haven't thought about that for years, assumed I'd long since left such lurid fantasies behind me. Yet here I am shivering: a little girl again who's alone and scared of the dark.

There's quite a struggle before logic returns, resumes control. How could anyone be in the attic? How would anyone get up here for a start and . . . I close my eyes. I sleep at last. No dreams of Paul – no dreams at all – just a blank screen.

I sleep until about dawn. A pale, sickly light seeps over me from my porthole of a window. Night has gone and so have all its noises. No strange creakings now. No sounds from outside either – not a ripple of wind or rain, not even a sudden surge of traffic noises. Surely I can't be the only being awake at this moment.

I shiver – this time because I'm icy cold. How can the temperature have dropped so suddenly? It's as if I've woken up in January – not the end of May. I huddle the blankets round me and if anything, I'm getting colder. You'd think the cold is coming from inside me. It's then I see my door handle slowly turn downwards. I feel a tightness at the back of my throat and the very flow of my blood seems to stop but I can't move, I suppose I'm paralysed by fear. The door gives a little click. A scream dies inside me as the door eases open. I lie there, transfixed. But then the door stops moving.

'Who's there?' I cry, suddenly finding my voice.

The door slowly clicks shut again.

'Who's there?' I cry.

Nothing except this vast overpowering silence. And all at once I have this strange tingling sensation which I always get when I feel I'm on the edge of something important. And I'm not scared any more.

Instead, I spring out of bed and open my door wide. A ragged light streams through the attic. Our attic. I peer round me, warming myself on its memories. How could I have stayed away? This is where I belong.

My feet sink into the carpet as I prowl round my territory. There's definitely no one here. But I did see that door handle move – the door open. I can't have dreamt that. Can I? I don't know. Everything's so confused since . . . I sit down on the sofa. More memories.

I look up. Something catches my eye. Paul's picture of a rose, I'd put it just above my spotlight, only now it looks as if it's shrouded in mist. And it's crooked.

I leap up to straighten it immediately. But just as I am about to touch it I see the picture starting to move of its own accord – exactly like my door had earlier – and actually straighten itself up again.

I blink incredulously. What's happening? Am I hallucinating or is there some unseen . . . I hear my heart throbbing away while I stretch out my hand towards the picture again. It's then I feel a sudden ripple of air and something cool curling over my hand.

Part Three:
Chapter One – by Dean

Caro's told you what she thought of me: a boring toerag with a planet-sized ego. Not surprisingly, I never expected to see Caro again. Certainly not socially.

So the night she came looking for me was something of a shock. And an embarrassment. It was Thursday – the night Gazebo invited me round to his house to watch horror videos with the lads. Gazebo isn't a total ernie – he's got some U2 records – but he's pretty close. And I know the kind of people he goes round with and I pretty well despise them all. But since my girlfriend had chucked me, (I was pretty relieved about that actually) and my best mate was dead, (I hate the way my mum keeps saying, I've lost Paul. I didn't lose him. He died.) I was pretty permanently in my 'life's crap' mood, and I somehow ended up round Gazebo's.

And it was toe-curlingly, mind-blowingly awful. About twenty of us lads were squashed round a TV set pouring lager down our gullets, as Gazebo fast forwarded each film until we came to a gory bit. You know that film, *Scanners*, and the scene where someone's head explodes and it's obviously just plastic. Well, we scrutinised that bit of it, frame by frame while this guy kept spitting in my ear: 'Just watch his hands . . . Now see his jaws go. Magic.'

We'd finally advanced onto a new clip featuring a pervy nerd who liked covering himself in other people's skin when the doorbell went. Gazebo charged out while I wondered idly if it was his parents back early. But no, they wouldn't ring on the doorbell, would they? Shame. Now that would have been a scene worth replaying.

Gazebo returned hissing: 'It's two girls for you.'

I glanced round until I realised everyone was staring enviously back at me, making pumping movements with their elbows.

'What – *two* girls?' I stuttered.

Loud laughter followed, although I hadn't meant to be funny. Then Caro and Vicky edged rather unwillingly into the doorway.

'Your mum directed us here,' Vicky smiled apologetically at me. 'Do you mind if we drag you away for a minute?'

'Okay, sure,' I said gruffly. I glanced across at Caro. I expected her to look at me in her usual way – as if I was some foul insect she'd discovered in her lettuce. She always makes me feel really gross, to be honest. But tonight her head was lowered and her body slouched against Vicky's. Perhaps that was what made her seem smaller than I remembered. And tired – very tired. Even her hair looked as they say in the adverts – 'dull and lifeless', especially against Vicky's blonde mane of hair. And I couldn't suss at all why she'd come looking for me. Surely I'd be the last person she'd want to see now.

Caro was instantly recognised as Paul's girlfriend and as I eased myself up, there was a rather uneasy silence, broken only by the gormo on the video screaming, 'I want your blood'.

Gazebo placed the video on pause and then gave his impression of a tortoise sinking its head into its neck as he muttered, 'Paul – he was a good bloke. You won't find anyone who didn't have time for him.'

Murmurs of assent all round. Yes, everyone liked Paul, especially when they were sponging money off him.

Caro briefly peered up to acknowledge these tributes. And I was shocked by how weary and strained she looked. I couldn't stop a surge of sympathy for her. It's hard to dislike anyone who's been hurt and Caro's injuries were horribly visible.

Gazebo saw us to the door. 'See you a bit later, mate,' he said.

'Yeah, sure.' But I'd already decided that as soon as I'd heard what Caro had to say, I'd go home.

We'd reached Gazebo's gate before Vicky asked, in a very friendly way:

'How are you, Dean?'

We'd spoken briefly at Paul's funeral.

'I'm all right.'

'That's good. Really good.' Vicky's one of those people who covers embarrassing moments by contorting her face into a smile. So much so, that her smile is rather like a nervous tic. She wrinkles up her nose a lot too. In fact, right now I was getting the full facial cabaret as we waited for Caro to say something.

Finally, Caro spoke. 'Do you mind if we don't talk here? What about . . . What about if we go to the fountain – because what I want to tell you is in confidence?'

'Okay, sure,' I said, growing more and more confused. What was going on here? Presumably Caro wanted to ask me about something to do with Paul. Probably she wanted to know how to dispose (horrible word) of his records. But surely she wouldn't want to talk in confidence about that. Yet it must be that. What else could it be?

Vicky gently linked Caro's arm. Vicky was acting towards Caro as you might to someone who's convalescing from a bad illness. I trailed about four paces behind them like a bodyguard.

Every so often they made conversation with me – well, Vicky did and I gave these really dumb replies. You see, I can't do social chat. I think I'm only any good at arguing with people. Just last night I went on for hours arguing with this guy about the Beastie Boys and this rap stuff and why I think it's totally lacking. But with any other kind of conversation, my mind just freezes over and I'm lost. As for being deliberately funny – I'm the pits at that.

Unlike Paul. You know something – I never once saw Paul get mad. Perhaps he burned his anger in jokes and wisecracks. I don't know. For we were total opposites.

I can get a bit heavy sometimes and go on a bit, (don't tell me – you've noticed) but Paul was light-hearted about everything – yet never in a bad way. Except if he hadn't been so bloody light-hearted the day he went off in that boat, he wouldn't have thrown his life away after less than 200 months. That's all he had. Not much is it? And it was all his own fault. He went too far out, and when the wind got up and overpowered his boat he didn't have a chance. Just before he left he was going on about his sailing and I said, 'Remember you're only an amateur.' But he just smiled, as usual.

The fountain is where weeny-boppers converge to strut about in their designer denims, and as it was a warm evening there were packs of them, ready to size us up.

'Hello, Dean,' called out one guy to me.

One circled round my belly button, his music blaring over us.

'I hate Gothics,' he said.

In a year to two he would probably be as big as the radio he carried.

'And I hate designer background music,' I said.

The guy looked at me in total bewilderment, before retreating, turning his music up louder as he went.

'I hadn't realised there'd be so many of them here,' cried Caro.

'The playground of the very brainless, this place,' I said.

Caro looked quite distressed at the quantity of morons round us until Vicky said,

'We'll go up a bit. Sit opposite where Mandate is. We'll be fine there.' Her voice was deliberately upbeat and reassuring.

I added, 'Yeah, we'll be all right there, for sure.'

We sat down. Caro in the middle. I shifted nervously expecting a discussion about Paul's records. I really didn't know what to do about them. But Caro didn't talk about records.

'That night when you came round,' she began, 'you spoke about there being proof that ghosts existed. And we argued about it.'

I nodded cautiously. Surely she didn't want to continue the argument now.

'And you said you'd seen a ghost – the ghost of your dog.'

I nodded even more cautiously.

'I was very rude to you that night, wasn't I?' Her tone was so friendly. I could only stutter in reply. Where was all this leading?

'Dean, would you tell Vicky and me now, what happened when you saw your dog's ghost.'

'Well – er . . .'

'I'd really like to hear about it. What was your dog's name?'

'Kelly.'

'Will you tell us about Kelly?' she smiled pleadingly.

Last time she'd barely even looked at me. And I thought her prickly, rude and far too possessive of Paul, if also very easy to look at. But now it wasn't just that I felt a bit sorry for her and she looked frailer than before. Rather it was as if she was in some kind of trance, for she seemed spaced out – not quite with it. I wondered if she was on tranquillisers. But she seemed to be getting worked up too, as if what I was going to say had great importance for her. But how could it? She'd never even seen Kelly.

By now Caro and Vicky were staring at me so intently I was uneasy.

'Well, my story is not anything sensational. It's just I had a dog, Kelly, a West Highland terrier. I'd take her for great long walks and she'd cadge food off me and most nights she'd sleep on my bed. Mum'd put Kelly in her basket in the kitchen. But the kitchen's got one of those doors you can't shut properly and most nights Kelly'd push open the door with her head, spring up the stairs and dive-bomb on to my bed. Sometimes she'd sleep downstairs for a while, then pound up to my bed about two in the morning and I'd wake up to hear her settling down beside me, panting right in my ear.

'Kelly leapt about like a puppy all her life. Well, until her last few weeks. Then she suddenly became very old, she had this chest infection and couldn't get her breath very well and she was always going down the vet's. Until one morning I woke up to find she wasn't on my bed. That was so unusual I ran downstairs. I found her lying by the kitchen door. She was dead.'

'Oh, that must have been awful,' said Caro.

'We buried her in the garden and Mum planted a tree to mark the spot. And that night I finally fell asleep about half past one. Only to be woken up by a very familiar sound. Kelly pattering up the stairs. The next thing I knew I felt something jump on the bed. I couldn't see Kelly but I knew she was there. I could actually feel her shape relaxing beside me. She stayed with me the rest of the night.'

'And did it ever happen again?' asked Caro eagerly.

'No, just the once.'

'Oh, just the once.' Caro looked disappointed. But I hadn't been. For hearing and sensing Kelly's ghost had scared the life out of me. And the following night – and many nights after that – I would shake with fear just at the thought of suddenly hearing Kelly running up the stairs. Or feeling her ghost settling down on my bed again. It wouldn't have been so bad in the day but in the middle of the night . . . For weeks I even kept this flashlight by my pillow. Poor Kelly – no wonder she never returned. But I didn't tell Caro and Vicky any of this.

'You're sure what happened wasn't – imagination?' Caro spoke as if she'd dredged the word up reluctantly.

'No, I don't think it was imagination,' I said. 'Similar experiences have happened to too many other people for it just to be imagination. I think there is proof for whoever wants it, that the body is just like a casing and when our body stops our energy carries on. Of course we can ignore the proof and . . .' I faltered. I'd said this before to Caro – that night in her attic with Paul. I'd been so confident then. I spoke as if I had death sussed – no problem. Total fake, of course.

But Caro's smiling at me, and such a wonderfully wide smile you'd think I'd just given her the antidote to all the pain inside her. Until I saw she was actually looking somewhere beyond me.

'Caro, tell him,' whispered Vicky.

'Yes,' Caro turned to me, smiling triumphantly. 'Yes, of course. Dean, you can't realise how grateful I am to you.'

'To me?' I gulped hard.

'You see, Dean, you've just confirmed something. Now I really can believe it.' She suddenly gripped my arm. 'Paul isn't gone.'

I could only gape at her incredulously as she went on.

'It's true, Dean. The first night I went home to my attic

I heard strange noises and saw my door handle move. Then when I was in my attic I saw something straightening the picture which Paul drew for me.

'For a moment I was very scared but then I felt a hand touch mine. I knew it was Paul's.' She paused triumphantly looking at me, expecting a reaction. But I couldn't begin to take all this in. It was as if I was thinking in some kind of terrible slow motion.

'Every day since then,' she continued, rocking slightly as she spoke, 'I've felt Paul's presence in the attic so strongly – and I've been really happy until I suddenly thought – am I imagining it all? I want Paul to be there, so I am creating him with my mind. I got really upset because it would be awful if it was me doing it all and not Paul himself. That's when Vicky suggested asking you as you're an expert on this sort of thing.'

'Well – no I'm not!'

'And also, I know Paul would like it if I saw you – and told you.'

I turned my gaze on to the window opposite me. It was full of dummies wearing suits. Only they were all headless. They had necks but no heads. Normally they'd look strange and eerie but not tonight. Now everything in my world is so out of sync they seem perfectly normal.

'What I've said is a shock isn't it?' said Caro kindly. 'And I haven't told you very well, yet how can you tell anyone anything so wonderful as this?'

But is it wonderful to think of Paul as a ghost, haunting Caro's attic? I don't know. It is possible. After all, I believe in ghosts. But not in Paul as a ghost. No, not Paul. I must try and be rational about this. Caro's probably imagined the whole thing – it's easily done especially in her state.

'Have you seen – anything?' I asked Vicky.

'No, not yet,' said Vicky reluctantly, 'but perhaps I

haven't seen anything because I scare easily. Anyway, its Caro who Paul wants to contact, not me.'

'Dean, do you think,' went on Caro, 'that perhaps Paul is trying to contact me for a reason?'

'A reason?'

'Yes. That perhaps he's trying to get a message through to me?'

At once they were both gazing at me for explanations. But I had none.

'Well, yes, perhaps.' I said weakly.

'But how can we find out?' cried Caro.

'A good medium,' I said quickly, wanting to move the focus away from me.

'Yes, yes,' Caro nodded, 'that's it. But how do we get one? One that's not a fake.'

'They wouldn't be in somewhere like Yellow Pages,' said Vicky and she giggled nervously.

'You could try a Spiritualist Centre,' I said. 'They test all their mediums. Check they're genuine.'

'How do they do that?' asked Vicky.

'Oh, get them to find out information,' I said vaguely. 'I'll write down the address of one, if you like. There's an Open Meeting every evening – seven o'clock, I think.'

I wrote in my pad and handed the sheet to Caro before standing up. I had to get away for a while, to think this out.

Caro stood up too – 'Dean, will you take us there tomorrow? You're not doing anything tomorrow, are you?'

I wasn't doing anything. Period. But I didn't know about *this*.

'Well – er . . .'

'Dean, *please*,' begged Caro. 'If Paul is trying to get through we want to contact him as soon as possible, don't we?'

She was looking up at me, feverish with excitement and

hope. Now she had a purpose again. But what if she was just fooling herself – which she probably was – then tomorrow night could be very cruel. I shuddered. And I'd be the one who'd taken her there. There was another alternative of course – that Paul really was in the attic, trying to make contact. I shuddered again. I don't quite know why.

'Please, Dean?'

How could I refuse?

'Okay, only look on tomorrow night as just an experiment.'

But Caro didn't hear the doubts in my voice. She just clenched my hand.

'Thank you,' she whispered.

In less than an hour we'd become if not friends, certainly allies.

I sat down again. There were more excited questions. Clearly they saw me as the leader of the expedition, (even though I'd never actually been to a Spiritualist Centre). Suddenly I was aware of myself pressing my feet down so hard you would think I was slamming my feet on imaginary brakes. And that's exactly what I wanted to do – slow things down a bit, to give me a chance to try and suss this out.

But it seemed there was no way I could prevent us from hurtling into tomorrow night.

Chapter Two – by Caro

I'm wearing my brown suede jacket with tassels – Paul always likes me in that – only I hadn't realised how much weight I'd lost and my jacket looks as if it has been borrowed from someone a size bigger than me.

I'm also wearing a pair of rolled-gold earrings – a present from Paul. It's only the second time I've worn them as the first time most of the gold rolled off, leaving a manky black lead stain behind on my ears. They're already making my ears feel pretty sore tonight, actually. But what does that matter?

Just before I leave my mum catches me.

'You're not going to that Spiritualist place are you?' she asks.

I know she hopes I'm dressed up for a date instead. In a way I am. But not the way she means.

'Yes, of course I'm going to the Spiritualist Centre. Why wouldn't I go?'

'Caroline,' she speaks very slowly, 'is this wise?'

'But Mum, if there's a chance of contacting Paul what else can I do?'

And Mum looks away from me and says quietly, 'Just don't expect too much from tonight, will you, Caroline?'

I don't reply. I can't begin to tell her how much I'm expecting from tonight.

On the train Vicky's staring at me really anxiously, and

56

a worried look keeps tightening Dean's face. I know they're both afraid tonight's going to be a flop. But what they don't realise is I won't let it be. If, for some reason, Paul doesn't 'come through' I'm going right up to the medium afterwards and ask her for a private sitting. I've no idea how much it will cost but I've brought my savings book containing £407.50 and she can have every penny. After all, what's money compared to knowing I haven't lost Paul?

I shan't tell Vicky and Dean that, though. It would only make them even more worried.

By the time we locate the Spiritualist Centre I'm feeling sick with nerves. I think Vicky and Dean are too. And while we don't exactly hold hands as we tumble through the swing doors we're huddling pretty closely together once we're inside. For we're journeying into the unknown and all we have to guide us are images from films.

A part of me is already imagining myself being led through long, dark corridors – perhaps by a cackling hunchback – and placed inside a vast room peopled by shadowy figures babbling in foreign accents and waiting for mysterious raps from an old round table.

Back in reality – an elderly woman straightens a pile of spiritualist newspapers bearing the headline *Woman walks who has no legs*, while we find the entrance fee. (Double because we are not members.) We give her the exact amount.

'Oh, many thanks indeed,' she gushes and directs us into a small, dimly lit room which contains a lectern, and two large chairs set upon a stage and rows of dark blue seats.

It looks like a cinema but smells musty like a church. It's also empty except for a woman slumped forward in the front row. Is she praying? Is she the medium?

We sit behind her whispering. We're all awed by the ordinariness of it all. From this shabby little room we're going to contact the other world? It's really hard to believe. I try and pick up the atmosphere. Is Paul already here? But all I hear is the bird-like beep of the cash-till outside and a woman hollering,

'If you catch your hands in them swing doors you'll know about it!' Childish wails a moment later indicated someone now knew about it.

'Caro, you all right?' asks Dean gruffly.

'Fine. I just can't believe I'm here.'

'But it's not at all what I expected,' whispers Vicky who's still looking round in amazement.

'These sorts of places often look a little mundane,' says Dean.

'See that chair,' whispers Vicky, (we're all still whispering). She points to a most uncomfortable looking chair squashed between the two other chairs on the stage.

'That was awarded,' she reads, 'to someone whose name I can't read. But it doesn't look very comfortable does it?'

'No, I shouldn't think he comes back to sit on that very often,' replies Dean.

Both Vicky and I smile at his little joke. Dean smiles then, highly chuffed. He's wearing a white shirt tonight. He looks so much better in smart clothes.

The room starts to fill up: a very aged man slowly manoeuvres himself into a seat behind us. He's accompanied by a stern-faced woman with freaky lips. She's streaked on so much lipstick her lips now resemble bicycle tyres. She sits directly behind Vicky, sighing so loudly Vicky starts giggling.

Then a red-faced man in green baggy cords and a yellow shirt bounds with surprising agility (as he looks all of sixty) to the front of the room. Rubbing his hands together he says, 'Can I have your tickets, ladies and gentlemen, please?'

'Ding, dong,' whispers Vicky, 'he thinks he's a bus conductor.'

58

For some reason all three of us start laughing louder and louder until I'm actually biting my hand to stop myself from laughing any more.

Suddenly the lights are turned up and there's a buzz of excitement. I turn round. The room is packed, almost full now and strolling up the aisle is a middle-aged man wearing a very neat moustache and a worn-out suit. He shakes hands with the ticket collector.

'It's a man who's the medium,' hisses Vicky indignantly. I'm pretty disappointed too. Somehow I'd assumed it would be a woman of about forty – with a soft voice and piercing eyes. And dignified – very dignified. Certainly not someone who says to the ticket collector:

'That's a flash shirt you got there tonight, Eric. I've dressed up too, you know. Wearing my golfing socks, got eighteen holes in them.'

Eric plunges his head back and gives a strange choking laugh. He's toothless – apart from two tiny pieces of white at the back of his mouth.

'You always make me laugh, Reuben,' he says.

I see Reuben's eyes darting round the room. He reminds me of a teacher from my middle school who used to make corny jokes and wear tired suits. Lived in a caravan, I think. I never liked him much. I don't like Reuben either. Surely he can't be the medium?

But then Eric starts rubbing his hands into a fine lather as he enthuses:

'Ladies and gentlemen, this is a very special pleasure for me. Tonight I'm introducing you to a really fine medium. In fact I think he's one of our finest mediums – Reuben Wilder.'

A beat or two of silence – no one knows whether they should clap – before Reuben says – 'Don't they look serious, eh Eric?'

Vicky whispers to me, 'He's going to be rubbish.' And I

notice Dean peering suspiciously at him. But no, he can't be rubbish – this is too important.

After a short prayer Reuben continues, 'I am here to reunite you with your loved ones and give you proof that there is life after death. The people I talk with are spirit people, not ghosts, not figments of my imagination. They are here because they want to contact you, give you a message. They are here now.'

Instantly we look round us. We can't see anything, of course – but presumably he can see a parade of – what did he call them – spirit people – gliding round this room. Is Paul among them? If only I could see him too.

'The spirit people need your help,' he instructs. 'They get rather excited and I can't always understand them. You must be flexible in your thoughts. It isn't always the people you expect who come through. You may get the lady who lived next door to you twenty years ago . . .'

I'm growing impatient. Enough talking. Just get on with it. At last he stops talking and paces back and forth. There's a hushed, aching silence.

He taps the wall. 'It's flimsy. Place is falling to bits, Eric.'

Eric laughs obligingly.

Then all at once he points into the audience. For a moment I think it's me but then I hear him saying:

'I'm starting by going right to the third row: there's a woman standing by the gentleman who like me has got a good head of skin. Did you ever know anyone called Lily, sir?'

'No I don't know anyone of that name,' the old man answers in a dry, rasping voice.

'I'm sorry, sir, it's not Lily, she's telling me off. All right! All right! No, it's Edith.'

'That's my mother,' whispers the old man.

'Your mother,' Reuben cries. 'Yes, that's who it is. Your

mother. Thought it might have been an old girlfriend at first – so that's why I checked. Now, what's that?'

Reuben's looking just above the old man's chair and nodding his head as if he's talking to someone. Is there really someone there?

'Your mother's saying something about March,' continues Reuben. 'Can you think why?'

The old man shakes his head.

'Did she pass into spirit then?'

'No.'

'What about her birthday?'

'No, that's in April.'

'Well, she's slipped a month. Anyway your mother loved you very much, didn't she?'

'Oh, she did.' The old man's voice is becoming muffled.

'And she says she's still watching you – keeping an eye on you.' Reuben chuckles, 'She knows what you get up to. And she says you've still got that mark on your back, haven't you?'

'Yes,' cries the old man. 'Yes, I have!'

'The things they tell you,' remarks Reuben. Then adds quickly, 'Anyway, your mother is here to thank you for being a good son to her and to tell you she loves you very much.'

'Thank you,' croaks the old man. 'Thank you.'

'Now I've got a young man here.' Vicky gives me a shaky smile while my heart beats so furiously I can hear it. It must be Paul!

'Says his name is Alan.'

'I can take Alan.' The woman in the front row waves a black lace glove in the air as if she's bidding in an auction. I sit back saying Paul's name over and over in my mind – as if repeating his name could make him appear.

'Now Alan's sniffing your perfume,' observes Reuben. 'Got any on?'

'No.'

'Well, he's wasting his time then. Come on, Alan, let's be having you. I can see you're going to be a handful all right.'

Reuben could be hosting a game show with Alan one of his contestants.

'Alan's your husband, isn't he?'

'Yes.'

'And he says you were married a long time?'

'Fourteen years.'

'That's right, and sorry, my dear, what's your name?'

'Kate Anderson – Anderson is my married name.'

'Well, Kate, towards the end Alan wasn't himself was he?'

'No,' she whispers.

'He's saying to me now, "I was proper poorly towards the end." But he's fine now. Skipping about all over the place and actually looking as young as when you first met him.'

All the time that Reuben is smiling you sense his small pale eyes are watching Kate very closely, while Eric keeps giving Kate these really probing stares. Why is Eric still there? Anyone would think he was Reuben's minder.

'You've just been wallpapering your new house haven't you? He's laughing about that. And there's a wedding coming up?'

She doesn't answer this one.

'Don't look so horrified. Thinks I mean her.' Reuben smirks at the audience. 'You may not know about it yet. But you will. You've just ended one relationship, haven't you?'

'Yes, that's right.'

'Ha! Alan says he's pleased about that. That relationship belonged in the dustbin.'

'That's true,' she cries fervently.

'Oh – and he asks have you been to the dentist yet?'

'Not yet.'

'Should do. Tooth at the back needs looking at doesn't it?'

She nods.

'And what's that? Right, I'll tell her. He says you've got to believe in yourself.'

'Thank you. Thank you,' she cries.

Another satisfied customer. I listen to several more satisfied customers. But – no Paul. Reuben's gaze always passes over me. I still can't make up my mind about him. His eyes aren't exactly unkind. They just don't give much away. And all those awful jokes – that just lowers everything.

Behind me the old man is snoring gently. The woman with the mighty lips shakes him. But he doesn't wake up. His face looks happy, though. Perhaps he's dreaming of his mother.

I look at my watch. Only a few minutes left. My shoes are pinching. I haven't worn them in properly yet. But their tassels match those on my jacket. And Paul always liked that. Everything I'm wearing is for him as I was so sure he would come through.

But what if I've just been imagining it? And Paul hasn't got a message for me – because Paul hasn't ever returned.

Now I think about it, it's only at night I can really sense Paul – in my attic. And after all you can imagine most things at night.

I remember when I was little I'd wake up screaming, convinced there was something in my cupboard, waiting to jump out at me. The cupboard was removed – but the terror just transferred itself to underneath my bed.

Of course, there was never anything there really. Just like now . . .

I look up at some flowers perched on a shelf above me. They're artificial. I hate artificial flowers. Only these are even worse for they look all faded. Sort of decaying plastic flowers.

'And he's dropping a rose into your lap.' Reuben's voice springs out of the gloom. I look up. He is staring straight into my eyes. And for a moment I wince beneath the power of his stare. 'He's young, very young.'

'Sixteen!' I cry. I know I'm talking too loudly and I'm shaking. I can feel Dean's hand creeping towards mine.

'Well, sixteen's very young to me,' says Reuben winking at the others.

'And he passed over very recently.'

'Yes, yes.'

Reuben touches his neck, nodding at the space round me. 'He says he couldn't catch his breath when he died.'

Dean's clutching my hand tightly.

'But he's all right now. Look at him he's putting his arm round you. Come on! Behave!' And right then I could feel Paul charging the atmosphere just as strongly as he did in the attic.

'You're his girlfriend, aren't you?'

'Yes.'

'I'm glad to hear that – he's giving you a cuddle now. And he says you've got his earrings on – even though they're really hurting you.'

'Yes – yes, that's right.'

'He says you never liked those earrings but you're wearing them tonight for him and . . .'

'Has he got a message for us?' interrupts Dean rather abruptly. Reuben looks momentarily taken aback.

'Ah, yes – he knows you too. That's right. Have you got a message for them? What's that? All right, I'll tell them. He says he's close to you, very close to you. He's there now, smiling away.'

Reuben lowers his voice, 'It's a wonder you can't sense

him yourself as you've got psychic abilities yourself, young lady.'

'I have?'

Reuben nods solemnly. 'And so have you.' He points at Dean who instantly lowers his head.

'Everyone's got something,' says Reuben. 'Only most of us keep it so deep down we don't think it's there. I expect at the moment all you think about is dating and boozing – I remember it well – but later you'll think about other things. So just remember it's there. Now look at that – he's dropping another rose into your lap. The rose is the symbol of love. And that's two he's given you.' Reuben smiles at me.

'So he must love you very much, my dear. And what better note for me to end on. I'm already into time and a half, aren't I, Eric?'

I don't remember leaving the Spiritualist Centre or even what Vicky and Dean said – although I don't think they said much.

All I remember is a wonderful sensation of feeling as if I were floating, high above everyone else. My feet, presumably, were still touching the ground but they didn't seem as if they were.

And outside I remember staring upwards into a very rich deep blue sky. I don't think I'd ever seen the sky look so magnificent before. It was that muzzy kind of light now and growing darker by the minute. But what did that matter: not even the darkness could hem me in any more.

Tonight I've travelled through the darkness into another dimension. Now I know for sure that Paul isn't lost to me. In fact Paul is closer than ever before. He's probably waiting there in our attic for me now.

And to think I learnt all this from a tatty little man who made even tattier jokes. But that's the point, I suppose. I'd always pictured mediums as extraordinary, set apart from everyone else. But you don't have to be special to have gifts like that. We've all got such gifts. Even me!

It's like my last night with Paul when that feeling of terror passed through me as I started to see Paul as a ghost. It was horrible and I had instantly shut my mind down so I couldn't see any more. But I'm sure that was a premonition. I'd somehow picked up that Paul would soon be dead. Only I didn't understand the feeling – I thought it was just Dean's ghost story getting to me and I couldn't save Paul – then.

But now I can ... It was then my wonderful idea formed. At the moment I can only sense Paul, but if that medium can see and hear Paul, why can't I?

It's such a brilliant idea I want to tell someone. Like Vicky and Dean. But they behaved so strangely on the train home – both looking as if they were waiting to be photographed they were sitting so still, their faces blank. What were they thinking? And why weren't they more excited? Shock, I suppose.

So I'd better not tell them what I'm preparing, yet. I'll get Paul to appear, first. Then I'll tell them – or maybe, even show them.

Chapter Three – by Dean

It was as if a giant armpit had just been shoved up my nose.

The local youth club reeked even more than I remembered. Not the place I'd have chosen . . .

I recognised most of the people: those blokes pulling foam out of the chairs and on to each other's hair were in my form, as were some of those clustered round the canteen. The canteen, incidentally, consisted of crisps and an old dear dribbling a yellowish liquid into plastic cups. Next door there were roars and cheers as well as continuous shrill blasts from a whistle: whatever was being played in there sounded well out of order.

A couple of blokes nodded at me – they'd both been at that mega-bad video party – I hoped they wouldn't come over. I'd obviously arrived too early. I was about to go outside again, just to unclog my nostrils, when I sighted Vicky, wedged in a corner with a guy in a track suit. I recognised him as Mark Edmunds.

The girls like him even though he's got a nose that looks as though it's been chopped off half way. I went over and he stood up.

'Just keeping your place warm, mate,' he said, but as soon as I sat down he squashed himself beside me as if he were playing chaperone or something.

'It's even worse than usual on Thursdays, here,' said Vicky.

'That's when they play for the five-a-side trophy.'

'Really,' I said, totally disinterested.

'Recovered yet from last Friday?' said Vicky.

'Oh, yes,' I said quickly.

'What do you make of it then?' asked Mark. 'Wouldn't catch me going to a place like that,' he added.

'It was interesting,' I said shortly, not knowing how much Vicky had told him. Some of it had impressed me – but most of it was just so trivial. None of the spirits said anything important. It was too simple and homely for me. And yet . . . it had seemed as if Paul *was* there. In a way. I turned to Vicky.

'How's Caro?'

Vicky leant forward, 'Dean, that's what I wanted to see you about. I'm frightened.'

I could sense Mark squirming when Vicky said 'frightened'. That word wasn't part of his vocabulary.

'I told Vicky that you'd say she's making a big deal out of nothing,' said Mark, laughing right into my face.

'What happened?' I asked Vicky.

'I rang Caro tonight. She wasn't at school again today – she's been off all week. Says she's got this really bad migraine. But after telling me that, she suddenly says you mustn't worry, Vicky, I'm not sad any more – I'm happy, very happy.'

'Did she say anything else?' I asked.

'No, not really but her voice sounded strange.'

'Strange?'

'Muffled.'

'Perhaps it was a bad line,' said Mark.

'No, no,' I brushed this aside. 'On the way home on Friday Caro seemed very strange – almost as if she didn't hear what we were saying to her.'

'Exactly. Well, talking to Caro tonight was like talking to someone who wasn't really there,' said Vicky. 'And Dean, there's something else that's funny: every night this week I've offered to go round and every time she's put me off. Says she's having an early night or something. And she keeps telling me to go out and enjoy myself – and forget all about her.'

'She probably just wants a bit of time on her own,' said Mark.

'But she has time on her own,' cried Vicky. 'It makes me shiver to think of all the time she spends in that attic. Her mum's dead worried about her – says she won't even come down at meal times. So Caro's spending all day sitting up there – alone. Or alone with Paul.'

'Now that's crap,' said Mark brusquely. 'Look, I had a lot of time for Paul – he was a good mate. And it made me feel bad, very bad, when I heard he'd drowned but . . .' He picked up his plastic cup and started squeezing it. 'But these things happen and you can't spend all your time moping about it. The way I see it once somebody's dead that's it and there's nothing you can do about it.'

'But last Friday,' said Vicky, 'we all spoke to Paul.'

Mark placed the now heavily dented cup back on the table.

'That wasn't Paul,' he said, so confidently that I retorted, 'How do you know? You weren't even there!'

A shadow of annoyance crossed Mark's face. 'I'll lay any odds you like, that was not Paul,' he said.

'Who was it, then?' I asked.

'It was that guy reading your minds. You were all sitting there thinking about Paul, concentrating really hard – and he picked up your thoughts. He's been trained to do that. But that wasn't Paul. I mean, come on, do you really believe that Paul flew off to that Spiritualist Centre to drop in . . .'

'It doesn't work like that,' I said.

'Mark,' said Vicky, 'Caro used to think like you. She even had an argument with Dean about it. But now she's had proof – we've all had proof that Paul is still around, looking over us.'

'And living in Caro's attic,' sneered Mark. 'Just answer me this, did any of you actually see or hear Paul at that seance?'

'It wasn't a seance,' I said. 'And no, we didn't hear Paul – he spoke through a . . .'

'No, I'm sorry.' Mark put his hand in front of me. 'Unless I actually see something with my own eyes I can't believe it. And it's my opinion Paul's not in Caro's attic or anywhere else and the sooner you face that the better.'

The sweat count suddenly increased as a group of champion footballers tumbled into view.

Mark shot up, 'Wait for me, lads,' he called. He turned to Vicky, 'The sooner you all forget this nonsense the better. Believe me.'

As he disappeared Vicky said quietly. 'He came over to ask me out – well, that's one way to turn a guy off you.'

'He'll be back,' I said.

'Oh, I don't know if I even like him,' said Vicky. 'I don't want to get tied down at the moment anyway. Listen, Dean, I'm going to ring Caro again. Have one more go. If I invite her out for a drink tonight, will you come too?'

'Well, if you want me too.'

'Oh, yes. She's more likely to come if I say you'll be there. She says she feels close to Paul whenever you're around.'

It's funny: me being Paul's best mate made Caro wary of me – when Paul was alive. But now he's dead it's given me a strange new status – with both Caro and Vicky.

'All right, I'll wait for Caro,' I said. 'It can't be good for her up in that attic all day.'

'No, and perhaps we might find out what's going on. I keep getting the feeling that Caro's shutting me out from something.'

Instantly I thought perhaps Paul really was there in the attic with Caro.

But I didn't say anything.

Vicky jumped up, 'I won't be long. I'll use the pay phone outside.'

I sat staring at the crisp packets and squashed cups, which decorated the table. One cup still had orange juice in it as well as four cigarette stubs. Everything looked so messy and pointless. How could people want to come here every week? But this is the real world – the world that we're so desperate for Caro to rejoin.

Vicky came back, looking flushed and excited.

'I finally got through to her. That machine kept refusing my 10ps – typical. Anyhow, she won't come out tonight – I didn't really think she would. But she was very interested when I said you were here and she wants you to go round.'

'What, now?'

'Yes, she sounded very keen.'

'But why?'

Vicky shrugged her shoulders. 'But it's too good a chance to miss, isn't it? And when you're round there – ask her to come out for a drink tomorrow night. You can make it then?'

'Yeah – sure. I'm visiting my great-aunt in Penn during the day – the one who's a medium.'

Vicky looked interested. 'To ask her about all this?'

'Yes, I'm not really an expert, you know,' I admitted.

'Well, you know a lot more than I do,' said Vicky. 'I'm really grateful to you. And so's Caro.'

I blushed and stood up quickly. 'I haven't really done anything. But I'll try and persuade Caro to come out this Friday.'

'And will you ring me?' said Vicky. 'Just a quick ring so I know Caro's all right.'

'Sure.'

'Good luck then, Dean,' said Vicky, after which we both smiled. It seemed absurd to say 'Good luck' to me. After all I was only going a few hundred yards up the road to visit Caro in her attic.

But as I rang Caro's doorbell I felt uneasy and nervous – and yes, frightened.

Chapter Four – by Dean

Caro didn't open the attic door when I knocked so I eased it open myself. Everything was in darkness except for a bulge of whitish light at the top of the room. 'Caro?' I whispered. There was no reply.

I edged reluctantly inside. Perhaps it was the absence of windows that made it so stiflingly hot. But there was something else – a stale smell: the kind of smell you discover when you're marooned in your room for days with only an illness for company. There wasn't a breath of air anywhere. And was it ever light in this attic? I doubted it. There'd always be a kind of darkness here instantly toning down any stray shafts of light into a permanent twilight. Like now. But the dinginess did call up my last night here. Memories like snatches of a film started running through my mind.

I peered down into the eaves. Paul had stood right there, plucking out records and proclaiming, 'This is only probably the best single that's ever been released.' He was mimicking me, sending me up as usual. Where was he now – was he down in those same eaves, lost in the shadows somewhere? Anything seemed possible up here. And anyway if Paul was – a ghost – this was surely where he'd be. For this was his territory – his and Caro's.

I wanted to believe Paul was here – even if the thought

also terrified me. I'm a ghost hunter with a very nervous disposition!

As I stepped in front of Caro's sloping bedroom door I heard a hair-dryer whirling away. A dull, monotonous sound – but oddly reassuring.

'Caro, it's Dean,' I called through the door.

'Oh, Dean – be right out – just make yourself at home.' She sounded light and friendly and normal. I relaxed – a little. But I couldn't ever feel at home here.

Even last time I'd felt shut up as if I'd been plunged into a deep vault. And it's a peculiar room – bright posters peeling off hospital white walls and such heavy, depressing furniture: a wrinkled old table complete with swollen legs, a wicker chair unravelling its murky brown twigs into the atmosphere. I didn't even like the large green couch much. Too lumpy.

I gravitated towards a tiny flare of light. In the corner opposite Caro's bedroom a spotlight streamed over a picture of a rose. No mistaking that scrawly signature.

But what an odd thing for Paul to draw. He hated doing still-life pictures at school. Sketches and doodles were his skill. And I much preferred them to this picture. It was very carefully drawn, but ordinary. Caro's influence, no doubt. She probably hated his funny cartoon figures. A little tincture of the old jealousy returned. She exerted such an influence . . . There was no doubt of that.

But then jealousy quickly evaporated, leaving only a tired sadness. For she'd turned this corner into a kind of shrine. On the shelf below Paul's picture was that orange beard he'd given her, some photographs and a small green vase. Only the vase had no flowers in it. How odd – I wondered if there was some reason why it had been left empty.

'Sorry.'

I wheeled round.

'My hair felt really itchy. Still does, actually, so I've probably got fleas or something nasty – but anyway . . .'

She had on a black dressing gown with a picture of Marilyn Monroe on the back but otherwise she looked nothing like the invalid I'd been expecting. Even in this smeary light her rich auburn hair sparkled and her face positively shone with ruddy health. In fact it was difficult to believe she'd been shut up here all week as she looked so well. Relief surged through me. Caro was all right.

'It's so good to see you,' said Caro and gave me a quick hug.

Last time we'd sat opposite each other here, we'd been glaring and needling each other. It took Paul's death for us to realise we weren't rivals but fellow supporters.

'And how's Dean?' she asked.

'Well, I've been to a youth club tonight and my senses are still recovering. I saw Vicky there. She's worried about you – and has now worried me about you!'

'But I'm fine, as you can see,' she cried. 'That's just Vicky, always clucking after me like a mother hen. Anyway, come and sit down.'

I felt my skin prickle when Caro leaned forward. There was no way round it, she looked tasty.

'My family think I'm becoming too introspective – that's a good word, isn't it?'

'A marvellous word.' I stared at her disbelievingly. She seemed so high and happy.

'But of course so much has been happening up here they don't know about.' Caro smiled at me, a smile full of mysteries, while a tremor of excitement ran through me. 'And it was easier to say I had migraines than explain why I was really up here. I feel bad about worrying Vicky, though. But there's no way I could tell Vicky over the phone – and I know Paul'd want me to tell you first.'

'What do you mean, Paul?'

Caro paused. I followed her gaze to the wicker chair which was perched alongside the couch. At once I started as the chair creaked; the way a chair creaks when someone's sitting down on it. And then another sound – as if someone was settling back in the chair. Yet that's silly. All chairs make such noises – it's quite natural and doesn't mean anything. Until Caro said – in a surprisingly calm voice:

'Paul is sitting, just a couple of feet away from us in the wicker chair. Can you see him?'

'No, no I can't,' I said quickly. 'Can you?'

'Sort of,' said Caro.

'What does that mean?' My voice sounded muffled and cracked, as my natural cowardice started asserting itself.

Caro kept her eyes fixed on the wicker chair as she said:

'After last Friday I came back here so excited I couldn't even speak to my family. For I thought if that medium – who didn't even know Paul – can see him, why can't I? Especially as the medium said I have psychic powers. So all weekend I sat in here concentrating very hard on Paul – but got nothing. I could sense Paul strongly sometimes – but that was all. Then on Monday I saw this shape – it was very blurred and unfocused, as if I had really bad eyesight. Yet at last I had something, even though it never became any more focused.

'Then a few nights ago I woke up to hear someone calling my name. At first I thought the sound came from the blackness out of my window; but then I heard it again louder, coming from the attic. I knew then it was Paul's voice – only he sounded different. Lost, unhappy, afraid.

'I burst into the attic and there he was standing by the wicker chair. I saw him as clearly as I'm seeing you. And he smiled at me, just for a moment, then he faded away. But I saw him, Dean. I saw him so clearly. Dean, are you all right?'

76

'Yes, it's just a bit hot in here, that's all.' I recovered myself slightly. 'And have you seen Paul since?'

'Yes – each time only lasts a few seconds. Not sure exactly how long. But it's a start isn't it?'

'And do you talk to Paul?'

'I've only ever heard him call my name but I can pick up his feelings.'

'How well can you see him now?'

'Very dimly. Just an outline really, but Dean, I know he's there.'

I started trying to breathe in deeply, only there was no air to breathe in.

'What did Paul look like when you saw him?' I asked.

'Just the same.' Caro's gaze was still fixed on the wicker chair. 'Same smile, same white T-shirt he wears and . . .'

It was then I stopped believing her. Or rather believing it was Paul. Surely spirits would have no use for clothes – certainly not T-shirts. Poor Caro. She'd been shut up here so long she was going a little crazy. I've got to get her out of here – for a while at least. I rubbed my eyes. A pulse beat fiercely in my head. I felt sluggish. I wanted to close my eyes. But I mustn't. I must stay alert for Caro's sake. Only it was difficult. It was as if the room was putting me under an anaesthetic.

What should I do? Ask her some questions? Faintly suggest other alternatives: like those times she saw Paul at night were probably dreams? Or that she wants to see Paul so strongly she's seeing him the way men in the desert see water. So the Paul she saw was only a mirage. Yes, that was it. But how can I ever tell Caro that – I certainly can't explain anything in here. I'll ask her to go for a walk, I need some fresh air myself anyway.

But it was Caro who asked me a question, 'Can Paul give you his present now, Dean?' She pointed to a pile of

77

singles, tied together with a blue ribbon and lying underneath the wicker chair.

'Paul wants to give you them himself.'

'He does?' My voice was little more than a squeak. Now what was going to happen?

Caro nodded at the wicker chair. Could Paul really be sitting there? I'd just explained away Caro's story but now, I wasn't so sure. Especially when I heard that creaking noise again.

And then all at once the records swirled into the air as if someone had picked them up. For a moment they hung there as if on a ledge while I stared incredulously, my heart thudding and thumping. Then the records didn't so much fly towards me as flow, rather as if they were gliding down a stream. Years ago I watched a pantomime, where this guy flew right across the stage and I was mightily impressed – until I made out the wires – but this time there were no wires.

They landed right by my feet. And for a moment there was a hushed stillness. I couldn't even hear my heart any more. It had probably stopped.

Caro broke the silence by crying, 'No, Paul, put them in Dean's hand. Hold your right hand out, Dean.' I obeyed, too terrified to even think what I was doing.

As the records skimmed upwards a cold draught of air rose up my ankles, to my knees and finally my hand. Colder ripples passed over my right hand as the records slid between my fingers.

I tried to steady my hand. Impossible. It was shaking dementedly and the records instantly belly-flopped on to the carpet with a dull thud, while my hand carried on shaking as if it was still receiving a giant electric shock.

Caro leant across, clasping my hand in hers. But her hand felt odd – very hot and so dry, you half expected it to flake away.

'Dean, don't be afraid,' she began.

I didn't stay to listen to any more. I bolted for the door, and stood outside, gulping in air.

Caro rushed after me. 'Dean – what's wrong?'

I didn't answer at first. I was too busy stocking up with oxygen. Finally I gasped, 'How did you do that?'

She smiled. 'I didn't do anything – it was Paul. Surely you can believe that – you who taught me that energy never dies.'

And I did believe in energy after death when I read about it in books. It made sense, then. But believing Paul was there, in the attic, that was something quite different. For this wasn't something I could know and then half forget. It meant . . . What exactly did it mean?

I started. Someone was calling my name. Caro nudged my hand, 'It's all right, it's only Mum asking if we want any tea.

'Yes, we both will, thanks, Mum,' she shouted back. 'Poor Mum and her cups of tea! But you look as if you need one. You go back inside and I'll fetch it up for you.'

'No, I'll come down.' It was silly but I didn't want to go back in the attic – just yet. Who am I kidding? I didn't want to go back in there at all!

But Caro insisted I sit down on the couch before I fell down. Then she sped away, closing the door behind her. I could still run out after her. But there was no need – she'd only be a moment. Nothing to worry about.

I tried to concentrate my mind on the domestic scene downstairs: Caro setting out the cups on a tray, perhaps getting some biscuits too. Her mum asking questions about me, her sisters scuttling about the place – none of them ever imagining that just a minute or two earlier I'd watched a pile of records fly across this room. While it was happening I'd been convinced it was Paul. But as soon as

79

the special effects ended, the doubts began. And I remembered something else: just a couple of feet from where I'm sitting – right in the middle of the room – we'd had our levitation session. And for a few seconds Paul had grown so light – he was weightless. It was as if he'd evaporated away into nothing. And that was all achieved by the power of the mind.

So the levitating records – couldn't that have been caused by Caro's mind? Perhaps Caro didn't even realise she was doing it. It still seemed incredible. But I knew as soon as I left here that would be the explanation I'd believe, the one that would let me sleep easier at night. But while I was here . . .

I squinted into the eaves. The shadows were growing longer. In fact it seemed as if they were slowly creeping towards me. I didn't exactly *run* towards the light switch – but it was pretty near.

Not that the lights made much difference. The darkness was too strong in here. Now that was a stupid thought – getting me all worked up again. I sat back on the couch. Caro'll be here any minute. I'll gulp my tea and leave. Getting late now, anyhow.

Suddenly I jumped up. That wicker chair – it had creaked. I'm sure it had. Or had it? But no, of course it wouldn't have started creaking, because Caro's not here. And she was the one making all these things happen. Even so I started backing away from the chair as if it was a mad bull, out on the rampage.

My eyes were caught by the spotlight bathing Paul's drawing. It seemed to be growing stronger, unlike the anaemic efforts around me. It was then I felt a breeze of cold air rush in front of me.

But there was no cold air in here only . . . It was very low, but my name was being called. And the voice seemed to come out of the spotlight.

A choked cry forced its way out of my mouth. I tried to say, 'Paul'. There was no reply at first, just a deep smothering silence which I could feel pressing down on my head and a delirium-like strangeness.

Then I heard the voice again, 'Dean', and as my eyes followed the sound I saw Paul. He seemed to step out of the light – or perhaps he only stood in front of it. I don't know. But what I know is, Paul stood there.

Only he looked so clear and solid – not musty or phantom-like at all. It could have been Paul come back to life, grinning at me in his blue cardigan and white T-shirt. He looked like a human – not a ghost.

I didn't move, perhaps I couldn't, and I had this strange, tingling sensation in my hands. But I wasn't afraid – not then. Tears pricked my eyes. Paul looked so real and I was convinced I could even touch him and my hand wouldn't just go through him. I thrust my hand forward, the rest of my body still so rigid I could have been standing to attention on a parade ground.

Then Paul stretched out his hand – but it didn't seem to move any closer to me. Instead, I heard his voice again. 'Help me', he said in the same low tone he'd called my name.

Only this time it sounded so close to me he could have been speaking right beside my ear.

'Help you?' I stuttered but I was talking to the air. There was only emptiness where Paul had been.

He hadn't faded slowly away, as I'd imagined, rather he'd vanished just as swiftly as he'd appeared. I kept staring at the white light – dazed, but oddly excited. Something Mark Edmunds had said earlier flashed through my mind. 'Unless I actually see something with my own eyes I can't believe it.' Well, now I had the proof I'd seen Paul – with my own eyes I'd seen Paul!

'Mum had to let Andrea make the tea. Of course she

took ages. There's sugar in the spoon. I couldn't remember if you had sugar or not.' Caro clattered the tray down. 'How are you now?' I turned round. And there was no need for me to say anything. Instead she whispered, 'You've seen Paul, haven't you?'

'He was there just by his picture.' My voice still kept shaking, much as I tried to steady it.

'That's where I first saw him, his power must be strongest there.'

'And he looked . . . so solid, so real.'

'Because he *is* real.' Caro clutched my hand tightly. 'I knew if anyone else could see Paul it would be you.'

I couldn't help feeling a little proud myself. 'That medium said I'm psychic – but I've never seen anything like this – I mean it was Paul exactly. Only,' I suddenly remembered Paul's message, 'he said, "Help me." Has he ever said that to you?'

'No, never.'

'What could it mean?'

'Probably it means to help him get through.'

I nodded but there'd been such urgency in his voice as if he was in real pain.

'I expect Paul wants you to help him stay longer too,' continued Caro. 'For his appearances always happen very quickly – just a few seconds – never any longer. And sometimes it's so frustrating. I mean, it's wonderful while it lasts but afterwards you feel,' her voice trailed away, 'worse than ever.'

'It's almost like a reminder of what we're missing,' I said. 'A tantalising glimpse of Paul and then nothing again.'

'But I'm going to get Paul to appear longer,' she said, 'until he is here all the time.' Caro's voice had become a flat monotone, almost as if she was hypnotising herself. 'Today I haven't been able to get him at all – not properly

– but tonight I know I will. I'll set my alarm for two o'clock; that's the best time.'

Her hand anchored in mine was even drier than before. I drew nearer to her. She was scorching hot. And close up her face didn't look healthy at all, rather it was flushed and feverish. Like this room, Caro seemed to be burning up.

There was something wrong with Caro, wasn't there? And something wrong here in this attic. Something unnatural. Had Caro somehow managed to turn this place into a borderland between this world – and whatever lay beyond? Was that how I'd managed to see Paul and hear that voice – which now I think of it, didn't sound at all like Paul's.

Or was it an hallucination? The doubts crept back. But this time I still wasn't sure, for if it had been an hallucination or whatever, it was extraordinarily vivid. I mean, Paul hadn't looked misty as I would have imagined him – if he'd just come out of my mind. Perhaps my great-aunt could explain tomorrow. Or perhaps no one could.

I wanted to leave but I didn't want to leave Caro. I felt afraid for her, to be honest. So we talked for hours about Paul while the lights grew even dimmer and the tea stewed – an irrelevance now.

As I was finally leaving, I remembered my main reason for coming round.

'Vicky and I hoped you'd come out for a drink with us tomorrow night. Go somewhere quiet – it'd do you good to go out just for a little while. Needn't be long. An hour or so?' I was virtually pleading with her.

'Yes, all right,' she said unexpectedly. Then she changed the subject. 'Don't forget Paul's present. You know Paul wants you to have them.'

'All right, thanks.' I stole one last glance at Paul's picture, even now half expecting him to materialise again. But the white light seemed to have shrunk again and shone over nothing but a blank space.

'Do you want me to leave the door open for a while?' I said. 'It's like a greenhouse up here.'

'Is it?' Caro said vaguely. 'I hadn't noticed. Oh, and Dean,' her voice became confiding, 'if Mum asks you about my migraine, say it's worse and I'm going straight to sleep – that way I shouldn't be disturbed tonight.'

I shivered. Why did those last words sound so ominous? I turned back, facing her again:

'I'll see you tomorrow night, then?' I said.

'What?' She seemed to have forgotten about tomorrow night already. 'Oh yes, but if – if . . .' she shrugged her shoulders. 'No, there's no point in trying to explain anything to them. They won't understand.' She sighed and then smiled faintly, 'Only we understand, don't we, Dean – we, the haunted.'

Chapter Five – by Dean

'What a wonderful surprise!' Aunt Kate (really great-aunt), looked both pleased and excited. I think she guessed from my phone call this was not a social visit – especially as I'd never called on her before, anyway.

'Come in. I expect you need restoring with a vital cup of coffee?' For as long as I'd known her Aunt Kate had been old. But she never seemed to become any older. It was as if she'd allowed time to burn her hair white and scribble over her face, but then said, 'No more'. And as she bustled about that tiny kitchen in her blue jeans and white shirt topped with a flowered scarf I decided she was my only interesting relation. My mum was only ever coolly polite to her, having quickly classified Aunt Kate as one of the loony ones from my dad's side. But, Mum conceded, Aunt Kate 'knows things'.

'Let's take our coffee outside, shall we?' It was more like an announcement than a question. I guessed Aunt Kate spent most of her time outside. But as she opened the back door a doggy whirlwind hurled itself on to my feet.

'Oh dear, I'm afraid she still gets very excited by ankles.' Aunt Kate clapped her hands. 'Daisy, no!' If anything, Daisy tightened her grip on my left sock.

In the end Aunt Kate had to wrench Daisy off me. 'Daisy, no!' cried Aunt Kate tapping her on the nose.

Daisy merely rolled her meltingly large eyes in my direction.

'I'd forgotten just how exhausting puppies can be,' said Aunt Kate. 'But you get used to having a dog about the place.'

'How old was Darcy?'

'Fourteen. We were growing old together but not this little one . . . Go off and play then,' she said to Daisy, who was squirming about in her arms. Daisy leapt to the ground and promptly dived straight on to my lap.

'Daisy, no. You don't jump like that.'

Daisy, as if to end any further discussion, closed her eyes. 'She's all right,' I said rubbing her silky head.

'Well, I'm not surprised she's tired,' said Aunt Kate. 'She's been digging up my fuschias all morning. As fast as I put them in she digs them up again. Still . . .' she smiled affectionately. 'Have you got another dog yet?'

'No, we haven't. Mum says it's going to be bad enough having Dad under her feet when he retires next year, never mind a dog too!'

'Oh, but you must. Biggest compliment you can pay Kelly – who was a beautiful dog – is to get another. I shall suggest that to your mother next time I speak to her.'

'By the way, Aunt Kate,' I said, 'my mum doesn't know I'm here today. I'm supposed to be at school, you see.'

Aunt Kate didn't bat an eyelid. 'Yes, I see,' she said.

'Only I wanted to catch you before you went away on holiday – I know it's probably very awkward with packing and . . .'

'Not at all. I always pack right at the last minute and am unlikely to break the habit of a lifetime today.

'Now, what's all this about? It sounds rather urgent, Dean.'

I proceeded to tell her everything, ending with what had happened last night in the attic. Sitting outside with the smell of lilac wafting over us and the sky a still pale blue, last night seemed to belong to another time zone. Talking about Paul's appearance was like telling someone about a dream I'd had.

But Aunt Kate never once interrupted, she kept her gaze fixed on me, as if magnetised by my story. And when I'd finished she didn't say anything, just sat there, very still. The only movement was Daisy stirring and causing a gentle itching on my hand as she started licking – or was it washing me – before going back to sleep.

So I gabbled on, 'I, personally, believe in life after death – or rather that when our body stops, our energy carries on. But I've always thought most ghosts are just like zombies, repeating the same actions over and over. I remember reading about the tape recording theory of haunting . . .'

Aunt Kate interrupted, half chanting. 'Certain moments contain such strong emotions they record themselves on the surroundings and these past events can be tuned into by certain people.'

'Is that what happened in the attic?' I asked. 'Do you think that Caro and I slipped out of the present for a moment and picked up Paul in a kind of play-back from the past?'

Aunt Kate didn't answer, just stared at me expectantly until I said:

'But then that wouldn't explain what Paul said – or the way that it seemed as if Paul was looking right at me, would it?'

'No, it wouldn't,' she smiled gently. 'I was about your age when I saw my first ghost. The ghost of my father – your great-grandfather. He'd only very recently passed over when I saw him standing by the side of my bed in his best black suit looking very agitated.'

'How did you feel?'

Aunt Kate chuckled. 'Lets say it's one of those occasions when I was very aware of my heart bumping away. And afterwards I wondered whether to tell my mother, your great-grandmother, but I decided it would only upset her. So I kept my secret to myself until the next night when my father appeared again. Same clothes, same anxious expression. By then it had penetrated even my thick skull that perhaps he was trying to get a message to me. So the next night I stopped all this nonsense of being scared and concentrated my attention on my dear father. And he came through again – this time though, he was pointing to the inside pocket of his jacket. Afterwards I found his best jacket hanging up in the wardrobe just as he'd left it – mother hadn't been able to sort any of his clothes yet – and in his inside pocket I found some papers. It was his will. Everyone thought he'd died without making one – but the day before he died he'd been into town and had the will witnessed. That was what he was so anxious to tell me.'

'And did you ever see him again?'

'Only once, the next night. The deep shadows had gone from his eyes and he was smiling. I knew he was at peace now and that I'd never see him again.'

'Where do you think your father went?'

'I don't know. No one really knows. That's the mystery that lies at the centre of all our lives. Perhaps the next world is somewhere so glorious we can never imagine it – all we can hope for here is the shadow of what lies beyond.'

She looked directly at me but in quite a kind way. 'I'll tell you what I do believe about Paul. The spirit of a person who dies naturally usually leaves right away to take up their new existence. But, if a person dies violently or suddenly – as your friend Paul did – he may be so bewildered and frightened by this transition that he remains earthbound. These poor, confused spirits often seek either a place reference or a person reference. In other words, they haunt a house or a person – seeking security there and being too afraid to continue their journey.'

'And you think that is what has happened to Paul?'

'Yes, I do. He's trapped himself with Caro and so is lost between the two dimensions. I'm afraid for him – and for Caro.'

'For Caro?' I echoed.

'Caro is in great danger,' continued my aunt. 'She has become a medium far too quickly. For it requires the most concentrated mental activity. To be honest, Dean, I have only ever dabbled. I've been too frightened to follow my talent through. You see, mediums – the best mediums – have to give up so much of themselves and I was never prepared to do that.' For a moment she seemed regretful.

'But Caro has what I suspect are considerable psychic powers. Many people have, you know – most never realise it. Perhaps Caro wouldn't have known if she hadn't lost Paul. But her love for Paul – and his love for her too – have led them to use their power to its fullest and together they have opened a door to another dimension. But psychic energy – like any other kind of energy – has to be disciplined.'

Daisy's head suddenly started twitching and I could hear tiny growling sounds – more like bleats really – but her eyes remained tightly closed. She was having a bad dream. Kelly used to get them too. Funny to think of dogs having nightmares. I rubbed her head, just like I used to for Kelly.

'This door to another dimension that Caro and Paul have opened,' I said. 'What's going to happen about that?'

'I fear for both of them if the door is not quickly closed. You must try to close this door, Dean.' I lowered my head. Aunt Kate's eyes seemed to be going right through me.

'Why must the door be closed?' I mumbled.

Aunt Kate paused. 'Dean, have you ever rescued a bird

that's injured? You nurse it back to health until one day the bird starts flapping its wings and you know it's time to release it and let the bird soar away from you? It's not always easy to do but you have no choice, do you? Because to keep a bird any longer would be cruel – as well as denying the bird its natural life. Isn't that so?'

'Yes, I see that. But the bird belongs up in the sky – whereas Paul belongs with Caro. That's all they want – to be together.'

She sighed heavily. 'And all I can say, Dean, is that there are cases, many cases, of people near death who see dead relatives or other loved ones waiting for them. I remember this little boy – he was only seven – and lived up the road from me. And I stood with his parents as he lay dying in hospital. But do you know, just before he died, he suddenly started getting excited and calling out, not for his parents but, "Nanna, Nanna". And I really believe he could see her there waiting for him on the other side. So perhaps one day Caro will find Paul again. But for now Paul and Caro must continue in different worlds. Their destinies are quite separate.'

As she looked at me I could sense such power and strength coming from her. I wasn't sure if it was this that was making me agree with her.

'Caro has helped Paul get over the shock of his sudden death and adjust to his new existence,' she continued. 'But now the kindest, most loving act she can perform – though also the most difficult – is to release him. He will never find peace until she does.'

'But Caro can never do that,' I cried. 'All she lives for is Paul's next appearance – that's become her life.'

Aunt Kate leant forward and placed her hand on mine. 'You have psychic gifts too – quite exceptional, I would say. You proved that last night when you were able to see Paul.'

'When he asked me to help him what do you think he . . .'

'Dean,' Aunt Kate interrupted, 'there really is only one way you can help Paul: persuade Caro to let him go.'

Chapter Six – by Caro

It all happened so quickly and I want to remember everything. I don't want any of it to slip away. That's why I'm writing it down now.

I'd set my alarm for 2 am as usual. I hadn't been asleep very long as I'd developed this nasty headache – all week long I'd been pretending a migraine and now I'd really got one. But when I woke up it was as if the headache had been smoothed away.

For I felt so good I couldn't believe it. There were no aches – or pains anywhere. In fact, there was no sensation at all. It was as if I'd lost touch with my body as my limbs felt so extraordinarily light.

I closed my eyes so I could savour this wonderful feeling of weightlessness. And all at once I had this floating sensation: it was wonderful. I felt as if I'd floated out of my bed and right up into the air. It was then I opened my eyes and gazed downwards on my body.

I was floating just below the light fixture, about five feet in the air. But here's the funniest thing I can remember, looking down on my body with this strange kind of detachment and thinking, 'so that's what I look like'. It was as if I were examining my sleeping form in some giant mirror, except in a mirror you only get a flat, limited view of yourself and now I could get a full view: my eyes were tightly closed and my body was so still I couldn't even see myself breathing.

But I wasn't afraid. Quite the opposite. I felt so happy and safe up here on my pedestal, where everything seemed so tranquil and peaceful. It was only down there I was afraid and lost. Up here was where I belonged, up here with Paul.

Then I found myself drifting – and that's exactly the sensation – away from my bed. It was as if I were being gently blown towards my door. And it seemed to be happening so naturally and effortlessly – it is only now I realise how extraordinary it all was.

Only when the door loomed up did I feel the tiniest flicker of fear. I remember wanting to close my eyes but finding I'd passed through the door before I'd had time to do anything. It was as if the door wasn't really there . . .

And then, just happiness and a sense of how beautiful everything was, flowed through me. It was normally pitch dark in my attic at this time, yet tonight it was covered in a veil of white mist. And as I soared through the mist I could already make out a figure floating in front of his picture.

Only this time I wasn't staring up at Paul, desperately searching for his outline, straining for some hint of presence. I was right in front of him. And even though I was sure I'd switched the spotlight off hours ago, light still hung about him.

And he was smiling. Paul smiled very easily. In every photograph I have of him he's grinning away. But every so often his smile would look so sweet and pure – as if it had come from somewhere deep inside him – it'd take me by surprise again.

And right then was one of those occasions – and it was as if I were seeing Paul for the first time. And so without really thinking I reached out my hand towards his. I wanted to feel the warmth of his hand against mine but all I felt was a tiny breeze as my hand passed right through his. Not quite believing what had happened, I tried again, but exactly the same thing happened. It was then I realised neither of our hands were there. Not really there. And we ourselves were just shadows.

The horror of that thought pulled me away from Paul and almost before I realised it I found myself being sucked back to my body. It happened so rapidly I can't even recall going through the door again. It was all less than a blur. I just remember sitting up in bed, feeling so angry and disappointed with myself.

It had been so wonderful until I'd ruined it. What did it matter that I couldn't touch Paul? And why had I shown such shock when our hands failed to make contact? My silliness – and that's what it was – had ruined a unique experience. For somehow I'd had what they call an out-of-body experience.

Apparently they happen to a lot of people. There was a woman talking on television; she had been operated on, for something very serious – but she told how during the operation she floated out of her body and had watched it all – from four feet in the air. She actually saw the doctors working on her body and all she thought was, why were they going to so much trouble as she was fine up there. And when she felt herself being dragged back into her body she cried on and off for a week because she didn't want to come back.

She'd also been able to describe details of her operation, which she couldn't possibly have known if she had been unconscious.

But I'll tell you something funny – when I came out of my body I never once thought about what kind of body I'd passed into. I was much more interested in everything round me. It's only now I wonder: it can't have been a human body yet it must have been something very similar because Paul recognised me instantly and I had hands like Paul's. They looked solid but were just . . . Why do I keep going back to that?

All I want is to be lifted out of my body again and float towards Paul and tell him what does it matter if we can't touch each other. Knowing we're together is all that counts. So I lie still, waiting for that sensation of weightlessness, the first sign that it is happening.

But I remain grounded. I even begin to wonder if I've dreamt the whole thing until . . . I hear a tiny muffled sound, more like a whimper than a sigh. I listen intently. It sounds like the cry of an animal in pain. What is it? It can't be Paul?

I run into the attic – but the noise seems equally far away. It's as if I'm just catching the echo of a much stronger sound.

'Paul, Paul is that you?'

There's no reply. But the crying noise goes on, sounding so despairing and lost. Is it Paul? What else could it be? But why does he sound so strange and distant?

I call his name over and over again. Then I sit, meditating on him. Why won't he come back and let me explain?

There must be a reason. Perhaps when his hand went through mine . . . I thought I'd just shuddered inside – but what if Paul had seen – or even sensed – what I'd felt. And now he thinks I'm repulsed by him.

Suddenly I sit up. The noise is becoming fainter, much fainter. Does that mean Paul isn't upset any more – or just that he's going further away from me?

And then the noise is gone and the attic only contains a very hollow silence. I lean back in the wicker chair, waiting for Paul to return but he doesn't and I fall into a kind of half-sleep until a hand gently shakes me awake.

'Paul!' I cry, opening my eyes eagerly.

My mum steps back two paces. 'Why are you sleeping here?' she asks, but without waiting for an answer she picks up a tray from the carpet and places it on the coffee table beside me. 'I brought you some tea and toast up. So how are you?' She sounds like a busy nurse doing her rounds.

I smile faintly. What would my mum say if I explained to her what happened last night? I suppose I can't blame her for not believing me. Would I have believed anyone who told me about an out-of-body experience a few weeks ago? Anyway, all I want is to be left alone so I can get Paul back – he sounded so strange and unhappy last night – he obviously needs me more than ever now.

But Mum does not leave, instead she hovers uncertainly before saying, 'I'd like you to get ready for school after you've had your tea.'

'Sorry, Mum,' I say promptly, 'but I'm still not feeling too good. My head's spinning . . .'

'Then perhaps some fresh air will blow your headache away. It certainly can't do it any good, cooped up in here all day.'

Her voice starts rising even before I can reply. It's as if she'd rehearsed all my arguments in her head already.

'No, I'm sorry, Caroline. I've tried to be patient and understanding with you. I know you've had a nasty shock but I can't take any more of this. Enough's enough.'

I draw in my breath and hold it.

'You've got to start going out again. Taking an interest in things. I'm not having you moping up here all day – it isn't good for you. It isn't right. Now I've ironed your school uniform.'

'Mum, I've got a bad migraine.' I'm almost shouting at her.

'No, Caroline, I'm not having you burying yourself up here any longer – and that's that.' She marches to the door like a teacher determined not to have any nonsense. 'There's more toast if you want it. Downstairs in half-an-hour, please, Caroline.'

I glare at her while tears of frustration gather in my eyes. She has obviously made up her mind that it's best for me – and her – if I go back to school. But she couldn't have picked a worse time. I've so much to do today. I need a few hours at least of uninterrupted concentration to locate Paul and check he's all right. How can I waste time at school?

But as if on cue Mum starts calling up her time check. I'd almost forgotten this part of my life: gulping food down, racing the clock, day in, year out. I bung on my school uniform but don't bother doing my hair which feels like straw, or putting on any make-up. What is the point?

Mum is hovering by my door again.

'How's your head?'

'Terrible.' I give her my nastiest stare but nothing can break her resolve. As she scuttles off I wonder whether to stage a faint or something. But no, Mum's not going to leave me alone up here, however ill I pretend to be. So what can I do?

'Caroline, it's 8.15 am.' That's the final time check which means I should be out of the door by now.

'Paul, I'm sorry,' I whisper. 'I've been forced back to school. There's nothing I can do – but I will be back. Paul – you are there, aren't you? You haven't gone, have you?'

But the only answer is Mum's, 'Caroline, it's time to go!'

And as I come down the stairs my whole family are standing at the bottom watching me – like it's the first time they've ever seen me walk. They can't fail to notice how ghastly I look but they've all been rehearsed – if not over-rehearsed – in what encouraging things to say.

Then Mum dismisses the twins while Dad says, 'I'll give

97

you a lift to school as it's your first day back. I'll pick up Vicky too, if you like.'

'It's all right. I'll walk, thank you,' I say icily.

'At least it's Friday. Just one day – be back here before you know it,' says Dad.

'But I expect you'll enjoy it once you're there,' adds Mum. 'It's just getting back into the swing of things that's so difficult but . . .'

I edge away from them. There are few things worse than my parents being hearty and fake-jolly. At the moment I hate them so much anyway I can hardly bear to look at them.

So I give them barely a glance as they wave me off. My eyes are starting to water, it must be the glare from the light. It's one of those very bright, very close days.

I stumble towards the shops, more than somewhat disorientated. I feel as if I'm stepping back into a routine I've abandoned years ago. It's like going back to infant school. I'm about to buy some chocolate when I notice two girls from my form giggling and pointing. I suddenly realise I am the object of their amusement.

I can't blame them. I suppose I do look a wreck. Why is everyone so critical of everyone else?

As I draw nearer they call out, 'How are you, Caro?' voices dripping fake concern.

'Fine,' I reply curtly, sloping away before they can register how ghastly I really look. As I look down I see I'm wearing the wrong socks. I've put on my dark blue ones instead of the standard pale blue ones. That means as soon as I step into school I'll be marched off to the deputy headmistress for a very grave conversation. And then there'll be all the questions, the glazed smiles and whispered comments.

And it's all so empty – and futile without Paul. That's it exactly, futile. Yet if I try to explain what happened last night how many of them would even listen? Dean would. And Vicky – though even Vicky – but the rest . . .

It's then I realise I'm walking in the wrong direction. I'm going away from my school and towards the youth club and the cinema on a busy main road. I stand by the main road, watching the cars shooting past and breathing in the ugly fumes and picturing my days at school. Then I sway back as if to escape the nothingness yawning in front of me.

And I think, instead, of that sound last night – such a sad sound. I can't leave Paul like that. Oh, why can't anyone understand? I go on standing by the road but now I'm not seeing or hearing anything, instead I'm held there by a thought. A thought that will not let me go.

Last night I floated out of my body for a few glorious seconds. The only way I will find Paul is if I do it again. Only this time why bother returning to my shell of a body? There is one way I can make sure I never leave Paul again. One way . . .

I step forward.

Chapter Seven – by Dean

Caro and Vicky were late. We were supposed to meet outside the Ploughman's Arms at seven o'clock and it was already twenty past. Not that it mattered – except it gave me more time to turn over what my aunt had said, and get myself all worked up again – as I had on the train home. So I concentrated my attention on my fellow teenagers clambering all over the seats. They were loud and nerdy – the kind who came in boxes of a hundred. Even so, I couldn't help envying them their fast-growing suntans. Now and again I've wondered what I'd look like bronzed. I was just speculating on the amount of courage needed to wear shorts which resembled cheap tea towels when I saw Vicky, half-running towards me. She was alone.

Something was wrong. Anyone could have sensed that.

'It's Caro,' Vicky struggled to get her breath. 'She's been in an accident.' I let out a low gasp, while my aunt's words raced through my mind. 'Caro is in great danger!'

Vicky pressed my arm. 'It's all right, she's not badly hurt. She fell in front of a car this morning just before school. The car missed her by a couple of inches. She grazed her leg quite badly and is still in a state of shock. I went round on the way here. I didn't see Caro because she'd only just woken up. But her mum kept me for ages. She said Caro must have fainted as she'd had a bad migraine in the morning. Her mum went on and on about how they'd offered to drive Caro to school but she'd insisted on walking. I think her mum felt mighty guilty, actually.'

'So Caro fainted as she was crossing the road?'

Vicky fixed her eyes on mine. 'That's what they think happened but I . . .' she wavered. I knew what she was thinking. I'd thought it myself ever since Vicky told me. But the very thought of Caro taking her own life made both our faces tight with fear.

I put my arm round Vicky. To my surprise she didn't stiffen.

'Let's go for a walk, shall we?' I said. We wandered down a winding pathway which turned into a lane dominated by skyscraper trees. Stinging nettles and lanky weeds with white flowers swished unwelcomingly against our legs as we ventured deeper into the countryside.

'Have you spoken to Caro today?' I asked.

'On the phone at break time straight after I heard. Caro sounded as she always does now, woozy and spaced out – and as if she was saying "goodbye" to me. And when I asked her why she didn't call for me this morning, she said she forgot. But how could she forget? She called for me every single day before.'

'Where exactly did she faint?'

'Now, that's another thing – it was by the cinema. So what was she doing there? That's not on the way to school. Her mum says she lost direction because her head was hurting so much. But I know that's not true. What are we going to do, Dean?'

I looked up at the pieces of blue sky, visible through layers of branches.

'I skived off school today, Vicky,' I said. 'I went to see my great-aunt – the one who's . . .'

'Oh yes, I'd forgotten about that. What did she say?'

'She said that when someone dies violently or very

suddenly, their spirit sometimes doesn't pass over right away, it remains earthbound.'

'You mean they're still here but we can't see them?'

'Yes.'

'That must be awful. No one knowing you're still here, people just walking through you . . .'

'But Caro has psychic gifts and has managed to make contact with Paul.'

'So Paul really is in Caro's attic?' Vicky looked both excited and frightened. 'But isn't it strange no one else has seen him?'

'I've seen him.' My voice had turned into a mumble.

'You have? But you never said. When?'

'Last night. It wasn't anything spectacular – and I thought it might worry you.'

'It probably will,' said Vicky in quite a serious voice before adding, 'but you must tell me. I want to know.'

For the second time that day I recounted my sighting of Paul while Vicky gazed at me in wonderment.

'I've always thought there was something else, you know,' she said. 'After all, so many people see ghosts.'

'About one in ten people apparently.'

'As many as that? So that just proves there is . . .'

'Another dimension to our lives,' I interrupted, and then felt immediately embarrassed. That sounded so pseudy. But Vicky fortunately had missed what I'd said and was exclaiming:

'But look where we are! Isn't that St Bede's Church, the one you stood outside during your ghost hunt? The one you told us about in the attic?'

I'd been so lost in thought I hadn't taken in where we were going. But there just ahead of us was St Bede's Church.

'Isn't it funny ending up here . . . and where is your school – the one that's haunted?'

'Just down here,' I pointed. 'We've come out on to the back of it.'

'There are so many ghost stories about this place, aren't there?' said Vicky.

'They stretch back centuries,' I said, 'to when the plague victims were buried here.'

A car swerved behind us, a boy raced out of the car and into the church. He was clutching a large white plastic bag. Very soon no doubt his voice would ripple forth ... Nothing very sinister about this place now except for a certain stillness ... You sensed things waiting here, waiting for the light to be sucked out of the sky, and their world to dominate once more.

'So what happens now?' asked Vicky quietly. She was sitting opposite the church, her hands clenched together.

'On the way home tonight I was thinking so hard about all this I nearly missed my stop,' I said. 'And I believe what my aunt said is our only solution. We've got to persuade Caro to let Paul go. We must somehow explain to Caro that it isn't fair on either of them to keep Paul earthbound. You see Paul doesn't belong here any more – it sounds really horrible put like that, doesn't it?'

'It does a bit,' agreed Vicky.

'But Vicky, that attic's not a refuge for them any more – it's a prison. They're both trapped up there, and neither of them is moving forward.'

'Perhaps they don't want to move forward?' said Vicky. 'If moving forward means losing Paul, I know Caro would rather stay just as she is. From the moment she met him it was as if she was under some kind of spell.' She sighed. 'And I can't see us ever breaking that spell.'

Vicky ran her hands through her hair as her voice rose.

'I really want to help Caro so much, but I can't get through to her any more. It's as if we're on different wavelengths now, and every time I speak to her she sounds further away. And it's going to get worse. I mean, look at tonight, we both ask Caro to come out and she tries to kill herself!'

'We must be very bad company.'

Vicky stared at me in surprise for a moment then burst out laughing. So did I. Our laughter seemed to echo as everything was so hushed and quiet around us. But it was a relief to laugh and it energised me, somehow.

I stood up, brushing off the midges which were diving on to my face.

'Vicky, we must at least have a go at persuading Caro. And I think we should do it now.'

'Now?'

'Well, my aunt said Caro is in great danger.'

'You mean she could try and kill herself again?'

'I don't know.' I didn't really want to admit that possibility. 'I just think we must go right away.'

'Do you want me to come with you?'

I was surprised at Vicky even asking.

'Of course.'

'All right, then.' But we were still in sight of the church when Vicky stopped and, looking over her shoulder, said,

'Dean, would you mind going on your own, tonight?'

'What's wrong?'

'Nothing's wrong exactly. It's just ... Oh, this sounds really pathetic but I've been having some bad dreams lately. Well, the same bad dream actually – about Paul.'

'Do you want to tell me about it?'

She turned round smiling. 'You sound like a psychiatrist. It's pretty silly, actually. I'm on this train, which is pulling out of Stevenage and I'm glancing out of the window when I see Paul on the platform. I call out to him but the train's already rushing past.' She paused. 'Here comes the weird part. You know how sometimes when you look out of a train it seems as if the lights are running past your window. Well, that's how I see Paul. His face keeps looming into view and then disappearing as if he's racing to keep up with the train. And every time I see him he's smiling, only it's a really horrible smile – as if someone had just stuck his lips in a certain position. Am I making sense?'

I nodded vigorously.

'And he's dripping wet. At first I think it's just water from the sea – funny how logical that seems in a dream – but then I see he's dripping pieces of skin away – it's peeling off him, but worst of all are his eyes. That's usually when I scream. For he hasn't any eyes, just sockets where his eyes should be.' She shuddered. 'It's a disgusting sight. And I'm struggling to get out of the carriage only I can't move while the face at the window seems to grow larger . . . like some awful mask.'

'A death mask?'

'Yes, that's it. It's a really horrible dream, Dean.'

'I can believe it. And you've had this dream a lot?'

'For a while every night. And sometimes I'd be sitting in this carriage, knowing it was a dream and yet not knowing how to get out of it. But the last three – no, four – nights I haven't had the dream. But if I go into that attic tonight, which to be honest gives me the creeps, I'm afraid the dream will come back.'

I gripped her hand tightly and tried to sound like a friend rather than a psychiatrist.

'I can understand that, Vicky. So don't worry, I'll go on my own. It's no problem.'

'I'm not walking out on Caro or anything,' went on Vicky hastily. 'And tell her I'll be round first thing in the morning. It's just at night, especially now I know Paul is really there . . . I mean, it is wonderful, but I'll think about that when it's dark and . . . Are you sure you don't mind going on your own?'

'Sure, it's no big deal,' I lied. Vicky hugged me, brimming over with relief. 'Thank you, Dean. If anyone can persuade Caro to let Paul go – it's you.'

By the time I reached Caro's house the light was becoming smudged. I could almost hear the darkness lapping at my shoulders. But however dark it was out here, I knew it would always be much darker up in Caro's attic.

I stood outside. My insides knotted with fear. What was I going to say? My head was pounding so much I was unable to think properly. I just knew I mustn't fail.

Chapter Eight – by Dean

'She should be awake, she was the last time I looked in.'

But Caro's mum was wrong: Caro was fast asleep on the sofa: her head had fallen forward on to her chest, and her hands hung lifelessly towards the carpet, while the darkness swirled around her like thick smoke.

It was even more suffocating up here than I remembered. And that smell – that stale smell was much stronger and seemed to come off the walls now. No wonder the posters looked ready to fall onto the carpet, their edges shrivelled and blistering.

I could understand Vicky fearing this room. You could almost taste the gloom and decay . . . There was something here . . . But who could be here? Only Paul, my best mate. Yet now his presence seemed to blight everything, especially Caro.

What a nasty, totally out of order thought. But easy to think, up here with its deep darkness, except for that pale unearthly light which only ever hovers over Paul's picture, that permanently lifeless vase – and the sweltering heat. Just why is it so blazingly hot up here? It's as if this room is closer to the sun than anywhere else. That's just silly, of course. But perhaps we are closer to something else in this attic, something even more blinding than the sun.

I took a deep breath. I must wake Caro up. I stood right

in front of her. She looked as if she was frowning, certainly not at all peaceful. Where had her mind taken her?

When you think of it, we spend about a third of our lives asleep, all those hours – all those years – in another world. You don't realise what a strange thing sleeping is until you watch someone else doing it.

I called Caro's name and instantly she sat up, opening her eyes wide – almost as if she'd been expecting me. But as soon as she saw me a look of disappointment flashed across her face, and I knew it wasn't me she'd been expecting.

'Dean, how long have you been here?'

'Just arrived.'

'Well, come and sit down a minute. I keep dozing off today. I keep dozing off most days, in fact.'

I sat down beside her. 'You gave us a bad scare today.' I tried to sound concerned – but friendly. I think I just sounded like a nerd.

Caro rubbed her eyes. There wasn't even the illusion of health about her now; her skin was a deathly colour and her face looked ravaged with tiredness. But worst of all were her eyes – they seemed to be sinking further and further into her head. It was as if I were staring into an old person's eyes: eyes that only wanted to fade into the past.

'I'm sorry, Dean. I didn't mean to upset anyone – especially you and Vicky. I just want you both to be very happy.' She smiled faintly then leant back as if the effort of speaking had exhausted her.

'Have you seen Paul today?' I asked.

Her face, drained of all colour, turned towards mine.

'I thought I'd lost Paul last night. It was horrible.' She spoke slowly. 'But after the accident I was carried in here and when Mum and the doctor finally left I saw Paul standing by the door and staring right at me with such a concerned look on his face. As usual, it was only for the briefest moment but he was more definite than ever.' Her voice started tapering away. 'There's so much else I want to tell you but I can't right now – you see, I'm so tired. And I have a great deal of work to do tonight. For I want to try and see Paul for a lot longer than before and I want him to know ...' she faltered. 'Anyway, it's going to require a great deal of concentration. Perhaps together we can both try and contact him – and make him stay much longer.'

She leant across and kissed me very lightly on the cheek. And as she did so I hugged her – I don't quite know why. I just knew I couldn't let anything happen to her.

And that meant I had to say what every part of me was dreading saying. But there was no other way. I couldn't go on watching her draw further and further away from us into her own twilight world.

'Caro,' I began, 'I saw my great-aunt today, the one who's a medium.' As soon as I released the words it was as if some invisible force was punching my insides. This was agony. But interest flared across Caro's face.

'Did you tell your aunt about Paul?'

I repeated to Caro – as near as I could remember it – exactly what my great-aunt had said. I don't think I added anything of my own. In fact my voice was so monotonous and unemotional it was as if I were reading back my French translation or something. And when I related my aunt's advice that Caro must let Paul go – my tone became a dead monotone. But it was the only way I could say these words.

After I finished I waited for the emotional reaction, for Caro to leap up and argue with me and proclaim she'd never leave Paul. I'd actually have preferred that response to what happened: Caro stirred listlessly, but never said anything. Not a word.

Almost indignantly I asked, 'Caro, did you hear what my aunt said? You must let Paul go.'

'Paul will never leave me,' said Caro softly.

'Yes, but . . .' I stumbled to express what I wanted to say.

'Dean, this is where Paul belongs.'

My eyes turned to the light around Paul's picture. It seemed fainter tonight, almost sickly. And whereas before I'd been able to sense Paul here, tonight I couldn't – or not yet.

I just sensed decay hanging in the air like dust.

'Caro,' I started again.

She gently interrupted. 'Paul and I want to be together; that's all that matters to us. Thank you for coming to see me, Dean, but I'm very tired.'

She didn't look angry or upset with me; her face was expressionless. But it was as if she'd drawn a shade shutting me out, shutting out everything in fact but her happy hypnotising dream.

And I didn't know what to do. I hadn't prepared for Caro to simply ignore me. Although I should have done. For this is what Caro is doing all the time now, she's withdrawing from everything, disappearing before our eyes until one day she'll vanish from our world and be totally swallowed up by the world in this attic. That is what she wants. But it's wrong, isn't it? You can't just check out of this life – that isn't an option.

A sensation of anger started to take hold of me. I wanted to go over to Caro and shake the life and energy back into her. But instead I cried:

'Caro, you've got to stop doing this to yourself.'

My answer was a series of creaks from the wicker chair. But this time it didn't sound as if Paul was sitting there – only as if the last bit of life was being burnt out of that chair.

'You're throwing your life away!' I could hear my voice trembling but Caro just stared, rather as you do when a noise temporarily invades your sleep.

My voice rose, hot and loud now.

'All right then, go to sleep – that's what you do all day, isn't it? You've no interest in anything. You've just given up one hundred per cent. But that's wrong. Knowing Paul lives on should make you live more, not less. But you're just existing in a kind of limbo and you're ignoring everything outside this room, and that's wrong. This life is important, you've got to connect with . . .' I stopped.

My words were having no visible effect on Caro, but they were on me. I felt a right hypocrite. Imagine me, talking about connecting with people . . . Now there's a laugh. That's the trouble when you start giving people advice – you end up sounding like the teachers in assembly. And I still hadn't said what I wanted to.

'I love Paul and I won't leave him!' I suddenly realised that Caro was speaking and giving me a long, concentrating stare. She went on in a high, reciting kind of voice. 'Now I'd like you to go and I don't want to see you again.'

'All right, if that's what you want.'

'It is. All you're doing is tiring me out with your bad thoughts.'

I flinched. Caro must realise it's been really hard for me to say those things to her. I only said them because I care. Feeling both hurt and oddly degraded I marched to the door, then wheeled round stung to a fresh, wild kind of anger.

'And what happened today was no accident, was it?' I said it, jeeringly.

Caro moved her hand slowly as if it was carrying a great weight.

She pointed at the door. 'Get out now and don't ever come back.'

There was a crack in her voice but her tone was dry and weary. Then she lay back on the couch, eyes closed as if I'd already gone. I looked round and shuddered. I wasn't welcome here now, I could almost pick up the waves of hostility. What did I care? I never liked this room. I always felt alien here. And whatever strange forces were here I wanted no part of them. I'd done my best to warn Caro. I'd done my best.

As I stood by the door I stole one last look at her.

The darkness hung over her like a shield. I was really glad I hadn't got to see Caro any more. I can't bear seeing her just wasting away like this. I heard myself release a last burst of anger. 'Caro, yes, you, sleeping over there – one final thing to tell you. You think you're being so brave and noble throwing your life away. But you're not. It's easy to love a memory, the easiest thing in the world.'

It was actually a relief to let loose some of the frustration which had been simmering inside me – until I saw Caro's reaction: she simply curled up tightly into a ball as if to ward off anything else I might say.

But I had nothing else left to say. And as soon as I stepped outside I knew I'd blown it. I'll have to ring Vicky now and tell her my operation to rescue Caro has been a total disaster.

Why had I been so bunglingly inept? How could I have got mad with Caro? There's a great gaping void in her life – any fool can see that.

Just as any fool can see Caro can't let Paul go because she only exists through Paul. She doesn't, of course – but that's what she thinks. And I've done a really pathetic job about persuading her otherwise.

On the way home I had a sudden, terrible thought: if I hadn't introduced Caro to the idea of ghosts and spirits could she have let Paul go more easily? Might she even have come to terms with Paul's loss by now? By telling her about Paul existing after he died haven't I just stoked up her pain? Could you even say I'm the one who pushed Caro into her negative limbo, Caro's so spellbound by the idea of contacting Paul, she's stifling everything else in her life.

But if Paul does exist in Caro's attic, surely she should know about it? Or might it have been better if she'd never known? For then Paul would have moved on and Caro – well, she'd surely be happier than she is now . . .

I kept repeating the arguments over and over as if they were some riddle I was trying to solve. And when I finally arrived home the arguments in my head were raging more fiercely than ever. Although I was pretty well convinced. It was all my fault.

Not intentionally though. I'd really thought knowing we survive death would be a kind of consolation. But it hadn't been the least bit consoling for Vicky, Caro or me. In fact, you could say all *that* knowledge had done was choke up our lives.

And now Caro seemed stuck in her half-life: sleeping through every day as she waited for the dark to push back the light and another half-second glimpse of Paul. I can't leave her like that, or Paul hovering in his no-man's world. But what else can I do? If only my aunt was here she might know what to do. Who else? It'd be no good asking my parents.

I dialled Vicky's number. I had to talk to someone, even though I dreaded telling her what a mess I'd made of things. But before Vicky's number rang I put the phone down again. An idea had hit me – just when I was thinking of something else. There was one other way, of course there was. Why hadn't I thought of it before?

Chapter Nine – by Dean

A woman wearing a tent tapped her foot impatiently. She turned to the two figures huddled conspiratorially in the bus shelter.

'Ten minutes late already,' she exclaimed. Vicky and I murmured sympathetically.

'I don't know why they bother with timetables – they're nothing but fiction. Buses just turn up when they feel like it.'

We made further murmuring noises but our eyes never left the house across the road. We weren't waiting for a bus . . .

Vicky spotted them leaving first. She nudged me to stay still. Not that I could imagine Caro sighting us. She had her head down and her mum was guiding her down the road the way you might a sleepwalker.

Caro would be at least an hour at the doctor's (so her mum had said). Caro thought she was just going to get some tablets for her migraine attacks – but it was going to be closer to a complete check-up and interview; not that I thought any doctor could really help Caro.

Once they were out of sight, Vicky and I darted across the road. It was as if we were two burglars, waiting for a house to empty so we could break in. Except Vicky had a key – which she handed to me.

'I told her mum I wanted to cheer the attic up a bit so

I'd better go and buy some flowers. Or perhaps a plant might be better. Flowers might remind Caro . . .' Vicky's tone was brisk and businesslike. But she didn't fool me.

'Anyway, I won't be long, then I'll keep watch. The twins are in town with Caro's dad and they won't be back until lunchtime, but if they should return early, just say you're helping me.' Her voice splintered away. 'I can't believe we're doing this.'

Last night when I'd eventually phoned Vicky, she'd told me Caro was going down to the doctor's. It had seemed such a brilliant chance. But now . . .

'Dean, we are doing the right thing, aren't we?' Vicky wanted reassuring.

'I really can't think about that now,' I replied irritably. I'd sat up most of last night reading about exorcisms. I wasn't impressed. Like there was one where you try to lure the spirit into a bottle and then proceed to cork him as if he were a genie. Then there were other ones where you say prayers and command the spirit to leave. I couldn't see me doing any of that. I wouldn't want to do it like that anyway.

'I'd better go,' said Vicky. But we both just stood staring at each other uneasily. It's the word exorcism: it doesn't belong on a bustling Saturday morning. Or perhaps it does. Scratch any surface and you'll find a kind of strangeness lurking there. We spend most of the time ignoring it or pretending it's not there, except late at night, when it's harder to pretend. Or moments like now, when you suddenly find yourself plunging deeper and deeper into that strangeness.

'Do you think Caro will ever forgive us?' asked Vicky. She certainly picks her moments. What a time to ask me that.

'Vicky, I doubt this will even work. It probably won't. I may not even be able to get through to Paul.' I was too

115

tensed up to be anything but sour and ratty. But then I added more gently: 'This is all my responsibility – you're just buying the flowers.'

For the first time that morning Vicky smiled.

And then she walked so quickly away she disappeared from view almost at once. It was best to move fast. If you think, you usually seize up and do nothing. I unlocked Caro's front door and sped up the stairs.

Then I charged up to the attic in the manner of a bullfighter.

'Here goes,' I said and that sounded so corny I laughed out loud. I could imagine Paul laughing at that line too.

I turned the door handle. The door didn't yield at all. I tried again but it was obviously locked. Well, that ruined everything.

I stepped back, just in case I spotted the key in a corner somewhere. But that only happens in films. In a burst of frustration I rammed my fist against the door and it moved – a little. So I pressed hard, really hard on the door and I heard a creaking sound from inside. Of course the door couldn't be locked – why hadn't I sussed that before – there was no lock. So something must be wedged against the door. But what? The couch seemed the most obvious. Yet who had put it there? It must have been Caro; but surely if she'd suspected anything she'd never have left the attic and how ... Once again I decided to postpone the thinking for later.

And I just kept pressing my weight against whatever was on the other side. And soon I could hear more of those heavy creaking noises accompanied by what sounded like groans and grunts, the kind emitted from wrestlers on Saturday afternoon television. And it was as if I was involved in my contest with the 'something' inside and I was winning. One more push and I should be in. I paused for a triumphant breath. Only it caught somewhere in my throat. For the grunting was continuing – even when I wasn't applying any pressure against the door.

I gulped hard. Where were those noises coming from? There must be a logical explanation. If only I could think of it. The gruntings sounded more like deep burping noises now. That was so absurd I wanted to laugh. I nearly managed it too.

Only then the sounds stopped completely. And somehow that silence was even more eerie. I glanced down at the stairs. They looked most inviting. Then I thought of Caro.

I ran at the door, threw myself against it and fell on to the carpet inside.

I sat up, gawping round me in bewilderment. How had that door given way so easily? I stared at the outlines of the furniture. Everything was exactly where I remembered it. Nothing appeared to have moved. Certainly not that dark carcase of a couch, so still and silent. Not a thing. But something must have blocked the door.

I groped forward. The heat was pouring over me the way it does when you open an oven door. And the darkness in here seemed almost solid now. In fact you wanted to reach up and tear off pieces of darkness to prevent it from pressing down on you so heavily.

Whatever Caro – and I – had unleashed up here was growing steadily more oppressive. How would it end? Would the whole room just suddenly combust? I'd read about people who did that, they caught fire and burnt away to nothing but a heap of ashes.

I shuddered. And then with a shock I realised the light over Paul's picture was much dimmer. It was as if it, too, was drowning under the weight of all the darkness round it. I shuddered again. There were certainly strange currents adrift up here now, and something about this dark, parched world . . . It was then I heard footsteps beside the door leading into Caro's bedroom.

Caro was here. That was my first thought. That explained how her couch had moved so mysteriously. She'd been up here all the time. But I was thinking in gibberish. How could Caro be here? I'd seen her walk down the road to the doctor's myself.

So whose footsteps were they? I fumbled for the light switch – this darkness even seemed to be getting inside my head. I must have more light – even of the slightest variety. But as my hands went to touch the switch a sound like a pistol shot cracked through the air and right inside my heart. Or so it seemed. I staggered backwards on to the door.

Sweat was pouring down my back and I wanted to run away. But I couldn't move. Just like you can't move when you're having a bad dream at night. And now it was as if my worst nightmare had slipped out of my mind and was wrapping itself round me.

I gripped the door handle firmly. All I knew now was that I was very afraid and I wanted to wake up, where there was light and fresh air and life.

But before I could leave – another noise crept towards me – a low moaning noise.

I stood frozen, transfixed by fear. The low moaning sound repeated itself and this time I knew it was edging nearer, coming to get me. In nightmares I usually wake up before this. I went to open the door, but instead, closed the door again. In that second it came to me. What a fool I'd been.

I stepped forward, almost confidently. Now the moaning sound occurred again. But it couldn't frighten me any more. For I knew who it was behind the darkness. Someone with whom I'd spent hours swapping ghost stories.

Someone who had just tried to recreate my worst nightmare.

I was right in front of Paul's picture when I heard an almighty crashing sound. It was as if a piano had fallen on to the roof.

Yet, I barely blinked. At first it had worked. I had been so overwhelmed by this rollercoaster ride through my worst fantasies that my mind hadn't stretched beyond them – to the source of these verbal fireworks.

It was the moaning which gave Paul away. That was his speciality. At the end of parties when the lights suddenly went out (and guess who did that) was Paul's favourite time, with French dictation classes a close second.

I smiled at Paul's picture. 'You always loved scary noises,' I said, 'but these are by far the best. Most impressive – how do you do them? Do you just think of a noise and it happens? Got any more good ones for me?'

But there were no more sound effects. The display was over. Paul knew he couldn't scare me off now.

'Paul!' I cried into the silence. 'Where are you? I want to see you.' And I really did. Somehow I felt closer to Paul now, than at any time since he died.

But nothing stirred, except me. I began coughing. The air was so parched up here. And I was starting to sweat again.

'Paul, it's me, Dean, your mate. Your best mate. What are you hiding from me for?' I was shouting quite loudly even though I was certain he was in this attic just inches away from me.

'Come on, show me where you are. Do another of your sound effects. Do one of your moaning noises. The ones you used to do in French when Gus said he was going to set homework.'

But there was only silence.

'Paul,' I called and then stopped. I'd sensed a tightening in the air about me, the slightest breeze.

'Paul,' I began speaking all in a rush now, 'I only want to ask you two questions. First of all are you happy here?' I paused. There was no response. 'Well, I know you're not. How can you be? You're nothing here now, except a mind. And while our minds are the best part of us, yours is just festering away, not being allowed to grow and develop as it should but . . .' I stopped. There was a tiny sound – the tiniest sound like gas seeping away. It was as if Paul was slipping away, losing interest in what I was saying.

'Paul!' I cried, but there was not even the faintest breeze around me. I yelled, 'And what about Caro – that's the other question. Is she happy? Well, I can tell you she's not. At the moment she's exactly like you – neither alive nor dead.'

A rustle of air told me Paul was drawing nearer again. So I spoke more quietly not really knowing where the words were coming from.

'Paul, Paul, you were robbed of life and I don't know why. Perhaps you will know soon. But don't let Caro be robbed too.' I paused briefly. 'Paul, you love Caro more than anyone else – so give her the greatest gift of all – GIVE HER LIFE.' I paused, looking up at Paul's picture for inspiration. And there I saw Paul's face reflected as if it were a mirror. He was smiling at me but a sad, tired smile I'd never seen before. I rushed to the picture. But he had disappeared.

'Paul!' I cried, suddenly panicking. 'Paul!'

There was only silence. A new silence. A silence that held nothing but endless space. I turned again to Paul's picture. Only the tiniest light there now, like the glow beneath the horizon before the sun sets. And before my eyes the light ebbed away until all at once it was gone –

blown out. And Paul's picture was hidden beneath a blanket of darkness again.

'Paul!' I cried, but I knew he was gone.

I seemed to buckle at the knees and drop down on to the carpet, stunned by the enormity of what I'd done. I'd expected a long struggle with Paul. Instead I just said four sentences about Caro – but it was as if they were the words of a spell. And Paul had disppeared so quickly; perhaps that was the only way he could leave.

So now they were free – both of them. I should be relieved. But instead I just kept wondering . . . Where was Paul now? I tried to imagine him – what's the phrase – 'passing over'. I'd always pictured it like making a giant parachute jump. Beforehand it must be mighty scary. I remember my grandad telling me how he had to be literally pushed off the plane the first time he went parachuting. But then when his parachute unfolded and he found himself flying into the sky he said it was the most brilliant moment of his life.

Was Paul experiencing such a sensation? Was he even now rising high and free, finally released from all his pain? Was he floating right up there – with the sky close enough to touch, just like he'd dreamt about? In my mind's eye I saw Paul soaring into the light.

But round me there was only darkness and doubts. Without quite knowing why, I took Paul's picture off the wall. This drawing which I'd never really liked was suddenly very valuable. It was all that was left of Paul now.

There are memories, anecdotes and – for me – old records, to bring Paul back. But to think of Paul only existing in the past filled me with a horrible pain. I had a tight, cramped feeling in my chest. Just like I had had before. It was as if Paul had died twice. And now this crushing pain again. I lowered my head into my hands and closed my eyes. I can see further with my eyes shut. Perhaps I might even see where Paul has gone.

'What are you doing here?' I jumped to my feet. Caro's voice was angry but her face only showed fear. 'And what are you doing with Paul's picture?'

I opened my mouth but the words came from someone else.

'Dean's been helping Vicky tidy up your attic to try and make it look a bit more cheerful.'

I nodded gratefully. For a second or two I'd forgotten my excuse. 'Yes, Vicky's just gone to get some flowers. She should be back soon.'

How long had Vicky been gone? It felt like hours – but my watch showed I'd been up here less than fifteen minutes.

'Really, Caro, there's no need for this attitude,' her mother nagged on. 'First you refuse to talk to the doctor and now you're being rude when your friends try to make things nicer for you. There's no call for all this . . .'

Caro took Paul's picture from me in the way you might gently pick up a baby. But her hands shook and her whole body seemed drained of life. I guessed she had been up all night trying to contact Paul.

Somewhere in the background, Caro's mum was telling how Caro had walked out of the doctor's after only five minutes. But she was talking to herself.

Caro had started pacing up and down, increasingly distressed about something. Then she let out a strange sound, a kind of strangled sob. My heart gave a lurch and then started sliding down my chest as it struck me again just what I'd done, while Vicky's question, 'Do you think Caro will ever forgive us?' rang in my ears.

122

Finally, even Caro's mother noticed how agitated Caro was becoming.

'What's the matter now, Caro?' she asked. Her tone was softer.

'I've got a headache,' said Caro suddenly. 'So please leave me alone.'

'Well, that's why we went to the doctor's to find out . . . Is that the phone?' She ran to the door. 'Can't hear anything up here. Yes it is.' She put her head back round the door. 'You and I are going to have a long talk, young lady.' She turned to me, 'Stay as long as you like, Dean.' She went to put the lights on but nothing happened. 'Must have fused. No wonder it's always so dark up here . . .' She went off muttering, towards the screaming phone.

Caro started walking round the room then stared at me, her eyes red with tiredness.

'You're a bad influence here,' she said. 'Do you realise I nearly lost Paul the last time you were in here? After you'd gone I saw Paul standing by my door and he was saying "Goodbye". I knew he meant it too, until I told him you just wanted him to go so you could ask me out.'

I started. That hadn't been the reason, had it? I like Caro, care about her but not in that way. That was just crazy.

'I'm surprised you even got in here,' Caro said. 'I told Paul to keep you out. But we'll never let you in again. You mess up the vibrations every time you come in here. So just get out. You're not my friend any more.'

'Yes I am,' I said quietly. 'And I'll be outside if you want me.'

I stood at the top of the stairs. I wanted to run home and put my headphones on and blot all this out. But I couldn't just run away. I had to stay and face Caro after she discovered . . . I had to try and explain.

Time passed. Quite a lot of time. Vicky arrived and was

talking to Caro's mum downstairs. Or rather Caro's mum was doing the talking while Vicky was murmuring reassuring 'I knows'. Vicky was trying to keep Caro's mum away from the attic. For it would be too awful to have Caro's mum blundering into things right now.

I leant against the wall, imagining I was at home playing U2's best album. I could actually hear each track in my mind, and I imagined Paul sitting back, really listening to it – the only time he was serious was when he played music.

The attic door opened. I couldn't look directly at the figure huddled in front of me and turned towards the stairs. I'd heard someone. I hoped it was Vicky.

'Paul's gone,' whispered Caro. She seemed bewildered and lost, like someone who's been woken up in the middle of the night.

I started talking into my hand as if it were a microphone.

'I didn't have to persuade Paul. I think he knew it was the right thing to do . . . He did it to give you life, Caro.'

As I said this tears filled her eyes and were streaming down her face. I took a step nearer to her. Her shoulders were shaking as if she couldn't contain all her feelings any more. And then I watched her fall into Vicky's arms, her hands still clinging to Paul's picture.

Part Four – by Caro:
Four Months Later

'Your mum's parties were the best,' says Vicky as we start to climb the stairs. 'I couldn't get over the care she took. Like the way the tablecloths always exactly matched the paper cups and plates.'

'And the party hats matched – and me too, if Mum could have her way!'

'And what about the food – all those lovely chocolate cakes – and the massive birthday cake . . .' Vicky pauses. We've reached the top. 'I'm only dropping in for a minute,' I say.

'Yeah, sure, just a minute,' says Vicky.

We both assume a casualness neither of us feels. I keep repeating to myself – like an actress uncertain of her new role – I'm just an older sister looking in on her twin sisters' birthday party in *their attic*. I emphasise those last two words: *their attic*. It's been *their attic* for nearly four months now.

Vicky opens the door. I let out a low gasp. The attic is in darkness, just like the last time. But I see ten tiny lights flickering uncertainly as they move into the centre of the table and I hear twenty shrill voices – plus Mum singing:

'Happy Birthday, dear Andrea and Niki . . .'

There is much blowing and I suspect even more spitting and then darkness. One or two excited squeals are released before lights beam down powerfully, lighting up every

125

corner with an artificial glow. I had not realised before just how many extra lights and lamps Mum had fitted up here.

A chorus of girls and two boys encircle Andrea and Niki, their hands outstretched for cake. Mum rushes up to Vicky and me. She is carrying a bucket.

'It's lovely to see you both here,' she cries, smiling broadly.

'It looks wonderful, just as I remembered it,' exclaims Vicky. 'I was telling Caro how you always gave the best parties.'

Mum beams proudly. I suddenly remember her hurt face when I told her I wanted my next birthday party at McDonalds. The twins were born just in time.

'I like to make things nice for everyone. Anyway, you both must have a piece of cake.' Andrea spotted us, and charged over with two very generous portions of cake nestling in pale blue napkins.

'It's a house cake,' cries Vicky. 'Sponge cake, butter-cream icing and sweets – just like before. Oh, some things are too good to change.'

Mum is turning red with pride. 'There's plenty more,' she says before lowering her voice. 'Anyway, will you excuse me a minute. A little girl has had a slight accident in the bathroom. I think I've mopped it all up.' She pats me on the shoulder. 'We're so glad you came.' Mum's speaking as if I've travelled from miles away, not up two flights of stairs.

'What's the accident in the bathroom?' asks Vicky, her mouth full of cake.

'Oh, it's only Anne Crawford,' says Andrea. 'She went down to the bathroom because she'd got this tiny, weeny drop of lemonade on her dress and then she starts washing her dress in the sink. Only she can't switch the tap off.' Andrea squeals with delight as if she's just told us a joke.

126

Niki joins in, for once as animated as her sister. 'When Mum went into the kitchen she felt these plops of water on her head.' The twins' giggling is infectious. 'It was the water from the bathroom coming through the ceiling. Mum's been hours mopping it all up.' Niki sighs exactly how Mum does. Then she grins excitedly. 'And Anne Crawford still won't come back,' says Andrea. 'Not that she need bother now – Alison Ford's eaten all her tea.'

A spate of balloon popping totally overwhelms the droning of Ben from Curiosity Killed the Cat while a small group of girls start closing in on the two boys who are both – for some reason – wearing identical jerseys and cords. Andrea and Niki quickly move back into the action but not before Niki asks:

'Does coming up here remind you of when this was your bedroom?'

'A bit,' I reply.

Niki turns to Vicky and says:

'Thank you for coming to our party. I do hope you are enjoying yourselves,' in such a gracious hostess voice that we both smile.

Then our gracious hostess hurls herself into the corner of the room and the first food fight.

Vicky smiles nostalgically, 'It's just exactly like your parties – everyone arriving so prim and sweet and then turning into hoodlums!'

I nod. It is a bit like stepping into a time warp, remembering myself before – before I'd even met Paul.

'And do you know what else hasn't changed?' I say. 'The way you stuff yourself with cake.'

Vicky immediately drops her plate. 'Why didn't you stop me? It's probably crammed with calories – funny, we never thought about our weight then, did we?'

'We never thought about a lot of things then,' I say. Adding, 'Paul would have enjoyed this, wouldn't he?'

Vicky flinches, just for a second. But I see it. Mum does the same, whenever I mention Paul. They obviously think that never speaking of Paul is the best way to help me get over him. They are so utterly wrong. I don't want to pretend Paul never existed.

Vicky says quickly, 'Yes, Paul would have been in there, joining in the food fight.' Then she looks at her watch.

'Caro, I'm going to have to leap away. It's four o'clock already and Tony'll be round for his tea at five.'

'Oh yeah, sure.' Tony is Vicky's new boyfriend. He's very nice, actually, and absolutely crazy about Vicky. I think it could be getting quite serious.

I take one last look round the attic. I've been silly to stay away so long. Nothing of the past lingers here any more. Nothing at all.

Half a sandwich sails in our direction. The food fight is spreading rapidly.

'Time to leave – definitely,' I say. We skulk out unnoticed and down the stairs.

'So what's your mum preparing for Tony's first official visit?' I ask.

'Oh, don't ask,' says Vicky. 'I told her it's dead casual. And you know Tony hates any sort of fuss. But I bet Mum's upstairs now polishing the silver – if not her tiara.'

'How long have you been going out with Tony for?'

'Four weeks, three days and . . .' she checks her watch, '. . . sixteen hours, ten minutes.' I look at Vicky. Yes, she's got all the symptoms. Well, it's about time it happened for her. I'm very happy about it.

We're at the door. 'You all right?' asks Vicky. 'You've gone all serious.'

'No I haven't. I'm fine. So we'll meet you both at eight o'clock by the fountain?'

'Great!' Vicky's still scrutinising me. 'Well, what are you going to do? Go back to the party?'

128

'No, I'll probably just ring Dean, remind him about tonight.'

'He won't need any reminding,' Vicky smiles. 'I bet he writes down in his diary every time he sees you.'

I know Vicky'd like it if I went out with Dean but it isn't that sort of relationship. He's a friend, a really special friend. Every day after Paul left our attic, Dean came round to see me. Every day. And I was so rude to him at first. So nasty. But he still kept coming back. In the end I saw how much he cared. I couldn't have got through these last months without him or Vicky.

I open the door. The afternoon is covered with a film of misty rain.

'Let me get you a brolly, Vicky.'

'No, no, it's all right. I've got to wash my hair anyway.' And one look at her flushed, excited face shows me she's hardly even aware of the rain.

I wave her off. And I stand looking into the distance long after she's gone. There was this same drizzle the day I met Dean's great-aunt. She's an incredible woman. We talked for hours, but there was one thing she said to me I'll never forget. As I was leaving she said: 'There isn't a greater or more precious gift than the one Paul has given you.'

I kept thinking about that and it made me feel almost as if I was holding each day in trust for Paul. That thought grew in my mind and it turned things round for me, gradually. At first every day was a fight. I kept wanting to run away and there were moments when all the pain came back with such force. But every day gets a little better. And now, today, I've been up into the attic again. Almost the last hurdle. I don't think I'll ever mind going back there now.

I shiver. There's a definite chill in the air. Only to be expected in October. Winter is on its way. I'll go inside and ring Dean. I want to thank him for those records. I just happened to mention to him that I've developed an interest in Motown and this afternoon he left a whole pile of Motown albums on my doorstep. He didn't even knock.

After I've rung Dean I'll look out what dress I'm going to wear – one of my new ones, I think – and then I might just have a little nap. You see, I woke up in the middle of the night again today. It's a hard habit to break. But it's all right, I just lie and wait for the dawn and that funny pink light.

And I think of Paul – and how lucky I am. For now I know Paul isn't lost to me for ever. One day I will see him again.

You could say I've learnt to dream forwards instead of backwards.

For Paul is out there, somewhere, that's what's important. And one day, wherever Paul is – that's where I'll be too.

Pete Johnson

FRIENDS FOREVER 1 : NO LIMITS

Jez, Jason, Cathy, Lauren, Adam and Mark have promised to stay 'Friends Forever'. But now they are leaving school. Their lives are all changing – and at Lauren's birthday party, Jason tests their friendship to breaking point . . .

Gripping, perceptive and frequently hilarious, this is the first book in a major four-part series about the sort of friendship everyone dreams of but seldom finds.

Also available: *Friends Forever 2 : Break Out*
Friends Forever 3 : Discovery
Friends Forever 4 : Everything
Changes

Pete Johnson

I'D RATHER BE FAMOUS

'I don't want to just fade away down some back street, with Adam, and then end up on a gravestone with no one remembering who I am. I want to make my mark, show everyone I'm here and sign at least a few autographs before I die.'

Jade is sixteen and a half, with a steady boyfriend called Adam and a sometime job selling videos. But it isn't enough. Jade's problem is that she has very little talent, but she knows she can be a TV presenter. All she needs is one lucky break. Then Jade hears a dating show is looking for applicants. Adam would go crazy if she ever applied. So dare she? Jade dares . . . and her life will never be quite the same again.

A warm, funny and touching story which looks at television fame and teenage life today with real understanding.

"Very entertaining." *The Indy*

"Well researched, enjoyable and easy to relate to." *Material Matters*

A Selected List of Fiction from Mammoth

While every effort is made to keep prices low, it is sometimes necessary to increase prices at short notice. Mandarin Paperbacks reserves the right to show new retail prices on covers which may differ from those previously advertised in the text or elsewhere.

The prices shown below were correct at the time of going to press.

☐ 7497 0978 2	**Trial of Anna Cotman**	Vivien Alcock	£2.99
☐ 7497 1771 8	**Kezzie**	Theresa Breslin	£2.99
☐ 7497 1794 7	**Born of the Sun**	Gillian Cross	£3.50
☐ 7497 1066 7	**The Animals of Farthing Wood**	Colin Dann	£3.99
☐ 7497 1823 4	**White Peak Farm**	Berlie Doherty	£2.99
☐ 7497 0184 6	**The Summer House Loon**	Anne Fine	£2.99
☐ 7497 0443 8	**Fast From the Gate**	Michael Hardcastle	£2.50
☐ 7497 1784 X	**Listen to the Dark**	Maeve Henry	£2.99
☐ 7497 0136 6	**I Am David**	Anne Holm	£3.99
☐ 7497 1473 5	**Charmed Life**	Diana Wynne Jones	£3.50
☐ 7497 1664 9	**Hiding Out**	Elizabeth Laird	£3.50
☐ 7497 0791 7	**The Ghost of Thomas Kempe**	Penelope Lively	£3.50
☐ 7497 1754 8	**The War of Jenkins' Ear**	Michael Morpurgo	£3.50
☐ 7497 0831 X	**The Snow Spider**	Jenny Nimmo	£2.99
☐ 7497 1772 6	**The Panic Wall**	Alick Rowe	£3.50
☐ 7497 0656 2	**Journey of 1000 Miles**	Ian Strachan	£2.99
☐ 7497 0796 8	**Kingdom by the Sea**	Robert Westall	£3.50

All these books are available at your bookshop or newsagent, or can be ordered direct from the address below. Just tick the titles you want and fill in the form below.

Cash Sales Department, PO Box 5, Rushden, Northants NN10 6YX.
Fax: 01933 414047 : Phone: 01933 414000.

Please send cheque, payable to 'Reed Book Services Ltd.', or postal order for purchase price quoted and allow the following for postage and packing:

£1.00 for the first book, 50p for the second; **FREE POSTAGE AND PACKING FOR THREE BOOKS OR MORE PER ORDER.**

NAME (Block letters) ....

ADDRESS ....

....

☐ I enclose my remittance for ....

☐ I wish to pay by Access/Visa Card Number ☐☐☐☐☐☐☐☐☐☐☐☐

Expiry Date ☐☐☐☐

Signature ....

Please quote our reference: MAND